Eclectic Hair

With

Granny and Me

Written by:
Dr. Gillian Richards-Greaves

Illustrated by:
Ramsey Diven

To order additional copies of this book, contact:
Xlibris
844-714-8691
www.Xlibris.com
Orders@Xlibris.com

ISBN: Softcover   978-1-6641-6095-8
         EBook   978-1-6641-6094-1

Print information available on the last page

Rev. date: 03/03/2021

Contents

Thank you!

My late grandmother, Mary Emily (La Fleur) Dillon

My late mother, Waveney Irma (Harlequin) Richards

Christy Greaves, David Greaves, and Josiah Greaves

Dr. Austin Chinagorom Okigbo

Dr. Mintzi Martinez Rivera

Dr. Stephanie Singleton

Dr. Vibert Cambridge

Dr. Pauline F. Baird

Dr. Kimani Nehusi

Ms. Donnette Richards

Mrs. Stephanie Freeman

Ms. Wendy Langhorne

Preface:

'Grandmothers' and Hair in the Black Community

Grandmothers and older women in general, serve important roles in Black communities around the world (Jiminez 2002: 523-551). Grandmotherly figures in the Black community are often known by names like Auntie, Big Mama, Granny, and Ma Dear or Madea. These elderly women often serve as secondary mothers who assist parents in caring for children. In the Black community, many believe that having a child validates a person's masculinity or femininity (Cutrufelli 1983). Therefore, becoming a grandmother is often viewed as an achievement, a blessing, and an invaluable gift. Moreover, for many women, having children and grandchildren is a form of social security, an assurance that they will be cared for in their old age and after they die and become ancestors (Bush 1990:105).

In many instances, grandmothers are the primary caretakers or "othermothers" of children. Grandmothers assume this role when biological parents become sick, relocate to other places to work or live, suffer with mental illnesses or addiction, or when they die (Collins 2003: 319). In times past, underprivileged children were also 'given' to older women who were childless or who asked for a child. Sometimes, elderly women also become "othermothers" to children who are not their biological relatives. For example, during enslavement, when Black children were taken away from their biological parents and relatives and sold to other plantations, older women took care of them (Close 2015: 63-78). The practice of grandmothers and elderly women serving as othermothers existed long before enslavement and continues today on the continent of Africa, in Black churches all over the world, and in every facet of the Black community. Grandmothers often play a unique role in imparting knowledge to younger generations. They are like human libraries who use their life experiences, trainings, and talents to teach younger generations important life skills. Farming, cooking, money management, childcare, study skills, good hygiene, and hair grooming techniques are some of the life skills that Black children learn from their grandmothers and elderly women in the Black community.

In the Black community, hair grooming techniques and the cultural significance attached to them are passed down from one generation to the next. Grandmothers often comb their granddaughters' hair and teach them to create diverse hairstyles. Many of these techniques began in Africa and were kept alive by Black people who continued to practice them, even when they were forcibly taken to various parts of the world and enslaved.

In pre-colonial Africa, hairstyles were very significant because they provided messages about the persons who wore them. A person's hair was an indicator of their social class, marital status, occupation, religious affiliation, and much more. Thus, for example, warriors, political leaders, traditional healers, married women, and royalty were all identifiable in their respective African communities by the hairstyles they wore. Among the Yoruba people of Nigeria, for instance, the *ilari* (messengers) of the *Oba* (king) were easily identifiable in public because their hair was half shaved (*ifari apakan*) (Dabiri 2020:170-172). Also, among the Yoruba, male priests wore traditionally female hairstyles to show that they were *awọn iyawo* (wives) of the orisha (deity) named Sango (ibid). Among the Maasai of Kenya, men who are *moran* (warriors) generally have long intricately styled hair, but the women tend to have bald heads (Johnson 2013: 16).

During enslavement, when Black people were forcefully taken from Africa to other parts of the world, they continued to style their hair in creative ways, primarily because they remembered how to do so. Moreover, they used hairstyles to conform to oppressive standards of neatness, maintain a presentable appearance, reject European notions of 'good hair' or beauty, and for many other reasons (Johnson 2013: 32-42). Sometimes, they were forced to conform to standards that stifled their hair creativity or concealed it altogether. For example, in 1786, during the Spanish colonial period, Tignon Laws were enacted by Governor Don Estevan Miró of New Orleans, Louisiana, in the United States of America. Tignon, sometimes called 'tiyon,' is a kind of head covering that resembles the *gele* (head-tie), worn by West African women (**see Fig. 2**). Tignon Laws were instituted to prevent Black women and other women of colour from dressing and behaving flamboyantly like white women. So, Black women had to cover their hair with a headscarf or handkerchief to hide potentially intricate or ostentatious hairstyles (Gillespie 1997: 238). Tignon laws were part of the larger 'sumptuary laws', which limited the consumption of food, clothing, and other items, in order to prevent extravagance. However, during enslavement, Sumptuary laws were really meant to maintain the social structure of society and keep Black women subjugated and separated from Whites. Therefore, the headscarf indicated that someone belonged to the slave class, even if they were not enslaved. This was particularly aimed at preventing lighter skinned Black women from behaving like or passing for Caucasian (Winters 2016: 78-82). Although Black women were prevented from displaying their creative, elaborate hairstyles, they circumvented Tignon Laws by decorating their headwraps with beads, colourful cloth, jewelry, and other types of ornaments.

Figure 2

Throughout history, Black people have innovated Black haircare technology and products. Beginning in the late 1800s, for instance, an African American woman known as Madame C. J. Walker, whose legal name was Sarah Breedlove, marketed cosmetics, and hair products for Black hair. She created the Madam C. J. Walker

Manufacturing Company and was listed in the Guinness Book of World Records as the first female millionaire in the United States of America. Madam C. J. Walker sold hair care products, such as hair pomade, which moisturized the hair and scalp, and helped to promote hair growth. She also popularized the use of the hot comb with wider teeth to straighten the hair of Black women, and even some men (Bundles 2001). Moreover, Madam C.J. Walker pioneered products and technology that resulted in Black hair becoming more eclectic and styles more creative. Today, there are many individuals and companies that support Black haircare and hairstyles. In 1993, for example, an African American woman named Lisa Price established a brand of hair care products called Carol's Daughter (Jones 2019: 108-9). Today, Carol's Daughter's products are sold in stores all over the world, as well as on online marketing sites like Amazon.com and hsn.com. Carol's Daughter became popular not only because it was supportive of Black hair, but also because it was promoted in the media by famous people like media mogul Oprah Winfrey.

Black people continue to create traditional hairstyles that were transmitted through centuries of enculturation. However, they also create innovative styles that celebrate their African heritage and send messages to the people around them. Black hairstyles continue to be indicators of a person's persona. Thus, for example, a person may not be a Maasai warrior but her shaven head may communicate that same courage, confidence, and fierceness. Black hairstyles and the meanings behind them are a conflation of Africanism, enculturation, assimilation, and other factors that affect continuity of Black culture. Moreover, Black children, especially girls, continue to learn about hair grooming from grandmothers and other older women in the Black community. Social media also plays an important role in the positive messaging surrounding Black hair. Thus, for example, YouTube instructional videos provide information on how to care for and style Black hair and wigs.

Black people continue to face hair discrimination at work, school, and in every sphere of society, but increased knowledge about hair as well as the discrimination against people who wear natural hair, are bringing about positive changes in attitudes towards Black hair. For instance, in 2019, a group of organizations in the United States created an alliance they called The CROWN Act, which stands for "Creating a Respectful and Open World for Natural Hair." The CROWN Act was first introduced in California and became a law on July 3, 2019. The goal of The CROWN Act was to eliminate discrimination against Black people based on their hair textures or styles, such as bantu knots, braids, locs, and twists ("The CROWN Act," 2019). The CROWN Act works to protect Black people from discrimination in education, employment, housing, and every other area. The founding organizations of The CROWN Act included Dove, the National Urban League, Color Of Change, and the Western Center on Law and Poverty. Today the alliance of organizations that supports The CROWN Act has expanded, and so have the discussions on the role of Black hair in society.

Eclectic Hair with Granny and Me highlights the beauty and diversity of Black hair. It encourages the reader to explore the history, culture, and function of Black hair in society. For each hairstyle, there is a discussion of how it is made, its function, its possible African origin, Granny Mary's and Penny's experiences with it, and famous people who wore it. Ultimately, this book encourages the Black child to feel pride in having eclectic hair. After completing this book, the reader will accomplish three main goals:

1. **Learn** about the history, diversity, and functions of Black hair and hairstyles.
2. **Understand** how Black culture is inscribed in, on, and through Black hair and hairstyles.
3. **Show** respect for the diversity and uniqueness of Black hair.

Introduction

Katabuli Village: Meet Granny Mary and Penny

Figure 3

Katabuli (pronounced Ka-ta-boo-lee) is a small coastal village on the western shore of the bauxite-mining town of Linden in Guyana, South America. The word 'Katabuli' is said to be an Arawakan word, but no one in the village seems to know what it means. Katabuli has a small population of about one thousand persons, who live in brightly coloured wooden houses built primarily by the male residents of the community. Katabuli is a diverse community that houses different ethnic groups like the Amerindians (the first inhabitants of Guyana), Africans (Blacks), East Indians, Chinese, Europeans, and mixed-race individuals called *Douglas*. Each ethnic group has its own unique cultural practices, but they also share practices that are unique to Katabuli Village and Guyana.

Katabuli Village has a lot of hills made of sand, rocks, clay, and mud. Some of the hills are covered in lush green vegetation, including coconut trees, prickly *awara* trees and *cocorite* trees, and many other fruit trees. In the low-lying areas of Katabuli village there is a lot of sand and clay of different colours. Tropical fruit trees line the streets, providing shade, nutrition, and obstacle courses for the neighborhood children. A diversity of aromas emanate from flowering plants, and fruit trees, such as *jamoon* trees with their purple, tart, grape-like fruits, notorious for staining children's school uniforms; mango trees that bear Buxton spice, long mango, and other species of mangoes; guava trees laden with 'red-lady guavas' (guavas with red flesh) and white-lady guavas (guavas with white flesh); and Star Apple trees with their dark-purple, fleshy, succulent fruits.

In Katabuli Village, there are also many creeks, rivers, and large lakes that were created when the land was blasted for bauxite, a mineral used to make aluminum. However, one of the most prominent features of the Katabuli Village is the 216-mile-long black water river known as the Demerara River. The freshwater Demerara River runs along the entire shore of Katabuli Village. The villagers use the freshwater of the Demerara River to complete their household chores.

Every morning, "before bird wife wake" (before dawn), the village women make the short ritualistic trek to the Demerara River, carrying basins (tubs) of clothes, dishes, and other household wares. Once at the river, each woman secures her spot on the wooden landing and begins her chores. As they *gyaff*, pronounced ghee-yaff (chat), some women brave the icy cold water to clean their dishes, and scrub floor mats, while others wash clothes by screeching them (rubbing them together with the two hands), scrubbing them with hard brushes, and beating them beaters (a type of wooden bat). As the sun rises, the village begins to bustle with the noise of school children, vendors, and folks going to work. Every now and then, the women's chatter would be interrupted by loud splashes from the cannonballs and swan dives, as the village's youths jump from the twenty-foot Katabuli Bridge to the Demerara River below. Although many Katabulians have in-door plumbing and standpipes in their yards, they still use the Demerara River, just like they have done for generations. This ritual gathering allows them catch up on the most recent gossip, share information, fortify friendships, and much more.

Just across the Katabuli Bridge, and a few yards from the Demerara River, is a large family compound with three houses. In the center of the compound there is a standpipe that provides water to the families on the compound and other neighbors when running water cuts off. The compound also has many trees, including five coconut trees, four guava trees, a mango tree, a Star Apple tree, a cherry tree, two orange trees, and a jamoon tree. The residents use the fruits to provide snacks or to make fruit juices, jellies, and other tasty condiments. Granny Mary lives alone on the western end of the compound in a small two-bedroom yellow cottage that was built by her late husband John. When she is not working outside of her home, Granny Mary spends her time relaxing in her rocking chair in her tiny living room.

Figure 4

This is Mary La Fleur, known to the Katabuli community as "Granny Mary." She is eighty years old. Granny Mary is about five feet, five inches tall, with slightly bowed legs and large busts that provide cushion to her warm, engulfing hugs. She often wears colourful head-ties that cover her wigs, which cover her natural, cornrowed salt-and-pepper hair. Her head-ties often match her brightly coloured muumuus, which keep her cool in the tropical heat. Granny Mary always wears gloves, above which are rings of indigo-blue skin. Whether she's going out or staying in, Granny Mary always looks prim and proper.

Granny Mary was born in a faraway place called Sandvoort Village, in the West Canje region of the county of Berbice, Guyana. After emancipation from enslavement, Africans in Guyana purchased land and established villages. Today, there are forty-one such African villages in Guyana, and Snadvoort is one of them. Although the British were the last European colonial power in Guyana, the Dutch that preceded them greatly impacted Guyana's infrastructure, culture, language, and history in general. The Dutch-English colonial history in Guyana is observed in Sandvoort Village, which is divided into two sections called Dutch Quarter and the English Quarter. Granny Mary Grew up in the English Quarter. Before emancipation, Sandvoort Village was a plantation, which was owned by The Society of Berbice, a Dutch Company, and grew cotton, coffee, cacao, sugar, and other items. Sandvoort Village was established in 1774, after the land was purchased by former enslaved Africans, who later diversified agricultural activities and implemented new opportunities for earning income. Many villagers later became balata bleeders, who 'bled' or 'milked' the sap or gum from bulletwood trees (*manilkara bidentate)* by making strategic incisions (cuts) into the trees. The gum or sap that comes from the bulletwood tree is called balata, a kind of natural rubber or latex that was used to make rubber balls and other items. Several of Granny Mary's relatives worked as balata bleeders, while others worked on the nearby sugar plantation and in other areas of agriculture. Granny Mary's father was a 'cane cutter' on the sugar plantation and her mother worked on her family's rice plantation. In fact, when Granny Mary was a child, she spent countless hours replanting seedlings and doing other chores on the said rice plantation.

As a young girl, Granny Mary preferred reading books to the strenuous manual labor of the plantations. She endeavored to become primary school teacher because she wanted to help the children in her small community. She often escaped house chores and make the half-mile run to Uncle Frank's house, where she would read exciting books and assist the neighborhood children with their Maths problems. You see, Uncle Frank was a headmaster (school principal) at the local primary school, and he always encouraged Granny Mary to study hard and be the best in school. He was not so fussy about her completing chores before reading.

After graduating from high school, Granny Mary completed the Teachers' Training School, and became a certified primary school teacher. While training to become a teacher, she married her late husband John (known as Grandpa John) and had two children Michelle and Frank. Grandpa John was also from Sandvoort Village, and was a skillful carpenter, plumber, and electrician. Granny Mary and her family relocated to Katabuli Village when Grandpa John accepted a job as plumber with Guymine, the local Bauxite company. After Grandpa John died of a stroke, Granny Mary continued living in the little yellow house he built for the family.

Today, Granny Mary is a retired primary school teacher and Headmistress (School Principal) of Katabuli Primary School. Every day, she wakes up before day-clean to complete her household and outdoor chores. In the afternoons, Granny Mary relaxes in her rocking chair to read, watch television, and entertain relatives, neighbors, and friends. Her favorite guests are her grandchildren, especially little Penny, who frequently stops by to *gyaff*, taste Granny Mary's delicious cooking, or get assistance with homework.

Granny Mary is soft-spoken but very knowledgeable. She seems to have an answer for every question, and her answers are often long, elaborate mini lectures. When Granny Mary speaks, she often uses proverbs, and switches from Standard English to *Creolese* (Guyana's creole language). A creole language is a language that was created from the blending of two or more languages over a long period of time.

Figure 5

This is Penelope Sinclair, known as "Penny," by family and friends. Penny is ten years old. She is 'African-Guyanese' or Black. Penny has dark brown skin with large almond-shaped brown eyes. Her bright, mischievous smile is accentuated by the space between her two front teeth and her deep dimples. Penny weighs about 75 pounds and stands at around 4 feet, 5 inches tall, but her small frame does not inhibit her athletic prowess and her competitiveness. However, one of Penny's most striking feature is her full head of hair, which is often styled in "two puffs and a plait."

Penny lives in the large two-storey wooden house on the eastern side of the family compound, with her parents and three brothers. Her father, Peter Sinclair, is a forty-year-old construction worker. Her mother, Michelle La Fleur-Sinclair, is a primary school teacher who teaches at Katabuli Primary. Penny's favorite pastime is *gyaffing* with Granny Mary and learning new things from her. Every day, Penny wakes up around 6:00 AM to complete her chores before going off to school.

Penny is in 4th Standard or Grade 6 at Katabuli Primary School. In the Guyana and the Caribbean, children in Grade 6 are required to take the high school entrance examination called Common Entrance. So, most Guyanese children begin high school by the time they are about eleven years old. In preparation for the exam, Penny and her classmates stay after school every day to get extra tutoring called "Lessons" from their class teacher. During the break between the end of school and the beginning of Lessons, Penny and her classmates often play local Guyanese games like 'Saul Out', 'Bu'n Down House', 'Chinese skipping', ring games, and cricket. Once she gets home after Lessons, Penny usually puts her bookbag in her room and runs over to Granny Mary's house to have tea and *gyaff*, pronounced ghee-yaff (chat).

Chapter 1

Eclectic Hair 'Trouble'

As soon as her mom opened the door, Penny ran into the house, past her mom, her ribbons in hand, and hair unraveled and free. The hairstyle she left for school with is clearly gone. Pouting, with the deepest furrows in her brows, she said, "Good afternoon, mommy!"

Puzzled, Penny's mom Michelle crinkled her brow and said, "Hi pumpkin, what's your story? Why are you vex?"

"Nothing mom, I just wanna talk to Granny Mary," Penny replied grumpily.

Noticing Penny's obvious discomfort, her mom retorted, "You can talk to me. What's wrong, honey? Why is your hair open like that? What happened to your 'two puffs and a plait'?"

Without skipping a beat, Penny said, "It's that coconut-head boy, Trevor. He's always bothering me and talking about my hair."

In a soft calming tone, Penny's mom said, "Don't mind him. He's just a silly little boy. Do you want me to talk to his mother about his behavior?"

"No, mom," Penny said, in a seemingly frustrated tone.

Penny's mom pushed a bit more: "I can report him to the teacher and …"

"Mom! No, thank you! I just want to talk with Granny Mary!" Penny replied firmly.

Penny's mom relented and said, "Ok, go ahead. When you get back, you and I will pick up this conversation where we left off."

"Ok, mom, Bye!" Penny said as she scampered out the door and down the steps. She darted across the compound and up to Granny Mary front door.

Before Penny could knock on the door, it swung open and Granny Mary greeted her with a broad smile and open arms. Penny ran into Granny Mary's arms and

1

hugged her. Granny Mary reached down and cupped Penny's face in the palms of her glove hands.

"Howdy, Sweet pea. What's bothering you, my dear?" Granny Mary asked.

Breathlessly, Penny said, "Trevor said I have bad hair. He said Jennifer's hair is nice because it is straight and lays down flat on her head. But she keeps her hair the same way every day. He said, "'Your hair is frizzy, and your hairstyles are crazy'! But I like my Hair! My hair is nice, right Granny Mary?"

"Yes, it is!" Granny Mary Said. "Even though it's open and scattered all over the place like a wild bush, it's still beautiful." Granny Mary laughed at her own comment, and continued, "Honey, black hair is beyond beautiful! It's ECLECTIC!"

"Eclectic?!" Penny asked quizzingly.

"Yes, eclectic," Granny Mary said. "Come, let's sit and *gyaff.* I'll tell you all about eclectic hair."

Granny Mary and Penny walked hand-in-hand to the kitchen. Penny quickly took a seat at the tiny wooden table by the window facing the road. Almost instinctively, Granny Mary stepped behind Penny's chair and began re-styling her hair into the usual 'two puffs and a plait.' Penny wormed her way backwards, adjusted herself in her seat, and handed her bubblies and ribbons to Granny Mary to add to her hair. After a few minutes, Granny Mary tied the last ribbon bow and gently patted the sides of Penny's head to signal to her that she was finished.

Granny Mary washed her hands in the sink and returned to the table. Reaching for the teapot, she said to Penny, "Come child, drink some bush tea and calm your nerves."

Penny relaxed and smiled warmly. "It's just herbal tea, Granny Mary. Just say 'herbal tea.' Ooh, lemon grass! I love lemon grass tea!"

"Anyway, honey" Granny Mary said, "Let's talk hair."

"But, granny, you still didn't tell me what is electric," Penny eagerly replied.

Tilting her head to one side, Granny Mary asked questioningly, "Electric?"

"Yes, you said, Black hair is electric," Penny responded.

Granny Mary threw her head back and laughed heartily. "No, my dear, E-CLEC-TIC! Black hair is E-CLEC-TIC. It is diverse. It has many different textures, colours, and styles. It *is* many things and can *do* many things. It's eclectic. You see, bright eyes, I knew the day would come when we would have to have 'the hair talk.' So, I have been collecting photos of Black people with eclectic hair and compiling this album for you. Sit here and drink your tea, and I'll go get the album from my old chest."

About ten minutes later, Granny Mary appeared in the doorway carrying a large photo album. Granny Mary sat down across the table from Penny and opened the album, which had countless pictures in it.

Figure 6

"Who are these people, granny?" Penny asked.

Granny Mary smiled warmly. "They are some of the many faces of eclectic hair. This is my show-and-tell about Black hair—eclectic hair. You see, just like Black people have many different skin colours, Black hair also has many different textures and styles. However, one of the things that makes our hair most unique is its naturally woolly texture. Unlike other types of hair, our hair naturally grows upwards and outwards. Our hair stands up without the help of static electricity, gels, or other substances."

Penny excitedly twitched in her chair and readied herself for her hair lesson. "How do you know so much about eclectic hair, Granny Mary?"

"I learned about what our hair could do from so many people and sources; like my mom who learned from her mom," Granny Mary began. "Also, I remember seeing Black hair depicted on African masks, on sculptures, and in magazines. You know, we reproduce what we see in our community, and so, we continue to wear eclectic hair. In Africa, in the Caribbean, in the United States of America, and all over the world, Black people continue to replicate older hairstyles while creating endless arrays of newer ones. You see, Lovie, Black hair can be anything and do anything. It's eclectic."

Granny Mary picked up the album and wiped the dust from it with her gloved hands. She looked at Penny and said, "You see, my dear, there are so many different types of black hairstyles, we can never cover them all. But the way I see it, eclectic hair falls into three main categories: natural hair, processed hair, and extensions. Many Black people can wear hairstyles from every category. Some people even switch from one category to the next in a single day, and some wear combinations of different styles. See what I mean by eclectic?"

Penny smiled and nodded approvingly, "Yes, ma'am."

Chapter 2:

Natural Eclectic Hair

"Ok, let's talk about natural hair," Granny Mary said. "Natural hair is hair that has its original texture. You know, the texture of hair a person is born with. Because our natural hair is woolly, we moisturize our hair and scalp by adding 'hair grease,' like shea butter, petroleum jelly, and other kinds of hair products to prevent it from becoming too dry and brittle and breaking. Ancient Africans used substances like palm oil and animal fats to 'grease' or moisturize their hair and scalp, but today we have many more options to choose from."

Granny Mary continued, "One of the most common natural hairstyles for men is the low, contoured hairstyle. To create this hairstyle, you have to use scissors, electric trimmers, or some other tool to cut the hair very low to the scalp. Back in my day, there were special straight razors that were used to cut the hair low. Most of the men in my family, our teachers, and other professionals in the community wore their natural hair in the low contoured style."

Low Contoured Hair

As soon as Granny Mary pointed to the photograph labeled "B", Penny exclaimed, "She has boy hair!"

Figure 7

Granny Mary laughed heartily, then said, "No, she also has low contoured hair. Women also wear this hairstyle, and like the men, they use scissors, trimmers, and other instruments to get their hair like this. Some women wear this hairstyle because it is easier to manage, and it costs less to upkeep. With the low contoured hairstyle, they don't have to spend a lot of money on hair moisturizers, styling equipment, or hairstylists to fix their hair. In many societies, a woman's hair is seen as her beauty, so women are expected to have a lot of hair or long hair. Some women who reject these beauty standards, often wear their hair in the low contoured style. Lupita Nyong'o, the beautiful and talented Mexico-born, Kenyan actress, often wears her natural hair in the low contoured style."

"Did you have low hair when you were young, Granny Mary?" Penny asked.

Granny Mary chuckled and said, "Girl, I told you I have had just about every hairstyle under the sun. That's why I have so little hair left now. When I was a little girl, I used to sleep on my back, which prevented the back of my hair from growing. You see, the back of my hair was short, and the front was long. So, when I was ten years old, my mother cut my hair into a low contoured style to make all of it even."

Penny thought for a minute, before raising her right index finger as if she were in class, "There is a girl in my school that has low hair. She looks strange to me. She doesn't have ribbon bows or anything."

"Well, you know," Granny Mary began, "in many parts of Africa, schoolchildren in elementary school and lower grades generally wear low contoured natural hair. Because the climate is generally hot, a low haircut helps students keep a neat appearance, prevents lice, and supports good hygiene. The low haircut also prevents complex hairstyles from becoming a distraction to learning. It is only when girls enter high school that they are allowed to wear braids and more complex hairstyles. Sometimes, also, girls wear *berets* (a type of hat) as part of their school uniform, so having low contoured hair makes it easy for their *berets* to fit neatly and properly on their heads."

Clearly impressed by the information, Penny let out a low, breathy "Wow."

"Ok, on to the next photo!" Granny Mary said, trying to move the conversation forward.

Free or 'Wild' Hair

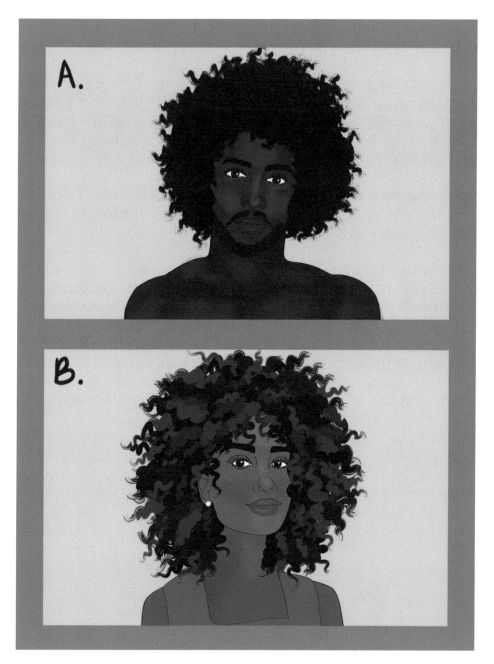

Figure 8

After turning the page, Granny Mary said, "Sometimes natural eclectic hair is free or 'wild.' You see how your hair was open and facing whatever direction it naturally falls? That is free hair."

Seeming a bit confused, Penny said, "But it was Trevor who messed up my hairstyle."

Granny Mary chuckled and said, "I understand. You did not want your hair to look like that, so to you, it was messed up. But some people deliberately wear their hair like that. The picture you are looking at labeled "A" is of Mr. Mike's son, David, a bright young man, and an amazing soccer player and sprinter. You can easily spot David during a soccer match; all you have to do is to look for that big head of hair. When he was younger, his father used to yell at him all the time and say, 'Boy, get rid of that bush on top of your head! You look like a senseh fowl!'"

Penny laughed. "Ms. Benn had a senseh fowl; all of its feathers were ruffled, and he looked untidy. Now, I really wanna see David's hair, Granny Mary! Can we go to his house?"

"Maybe someday," Granny Mary replied. "He is in the United States studying sports medicine. If he still has his big hair when he returns, you'll certainly get to see it."

Granny Mary pointed to the photo labeled "B" and said, "This is a picture of Debbie. She lives down the river and used to go to school with your mom, Michelle. She also has free hair, although her hair is a slightly different texture than David's. Debbie is *Dougla*. She is a mixture of African (Black) and East Indian, so her hair is not as thick and woolly as David's."

Penny reached over and turned the page to reveal the next photograph. "Wow! He has beautiful round hair. It looks almost like a hat!"

Afro Hairstyle

Figure 9

Granny Mary chuckled and said, "This hairstyle is called an *afro*. The term 'Afro' is comes from the word 'African,' one of many words used to describe people born on the continent of Africa; however, the term was originally used to refer to darker-skinned peoples. In the United States, where the afro hairstyle was popularized in the 1960s and 1970s, 'afro' refers to Afro-American (African American or Black American). The afro is a round-shaped hairstyle that is created with the natural hair. Actually, this kind of eclectic hair is also free, but I like to think of it as 'organized free hair.' It is big and open, but it is also molded."

"I've seen afros before, but how did he get it round like that?" Penny asked quizzingly.

"Well to get an afro you must first use an *afro comb* to comb out your hair," Granny Mary stated. "The afro comb, which some people call an afro pick, looks like a fork. Once you are done combing out your hair with the afro comb, you have to use a lightweight flat object, like a thin book, and gently pat the hair into the rounded shape."

Staring intently at Granny Mary, Penny questioned, "I wonder who came up with the idea of wearing big afro hair and combing it with something that looks like a fork." Penny struggled to control her giggles, as the dimples in her face deepened.

"You know, lovie," Granny Mary began, "although we sometimes think of the afro comb as a recent invention, archaeological and historical records show that afro combs were used in ancient Egypt. In fact, the oldest Egyptian afro comb is 5,500 years old. Moreover, archaeological materials from all over Africa show that hair combs were very important in many African societies, long before the afro comb became popular in this part of the Western Hemisphere. As early as 3500 BCE (Before Common Era), in the predynastic period, some of the earliest hair combs were discovered in Ancient Sudan and Egypt."

Penny interjected, "How did people get all that information about afro combs?"

Granny Mary nodded approvingly and continued, "Archaeological records, especially from burials, show hair combs of different types and sizes, which provided information about the people who used them. Also, beginning in the 1800s, missionaries and others who traveled to Africa, collected different types of hair combs. African hair combs had designs of humans, animals, and other objects in nature and the spirit world. The designs on the combs often highlighted the identities of the persons who used them, such as their tribes (ethnic groups), social statuses, and religious beliefs."

"Social statuses? Like if the person is rich or poor, or a king?" Penny asked.

"Precisely," Granny Mary said, vigorously nodding her head.

Granny Mary sipped some tea and continued her mini lecture. "During the Civil Rights Movement of the 1960s and the Black Power Movement of the 1970s, many Black people in the United States and around the world began wearing afros, and the modern-day, long-teeth afro comb became popular. The long-teeth afro comb we use today was first patented in 1960 by two African Americans named Samuel H. Bundles Jr., and Henry M. Childrey. Then, between 1970 and 1980, more than thirteen additional designs for afro combs were patented in the United States of America (Tulloch 2008). By the 1980s, many afro combs were made with the clenched fist, which was symbolic of the Black Power Movement that began in the 1970s. The first clenched-fist afro comb was patented in 1972 by Anthony R Romani. Then, by the 1980s, there were folding afro combs, which were red, black, and green, the colours of the Black Power movement, the pan-African flag, and pan-African identity. The patent for the folding afro comb was filed in 1970 and was granted in 1971. However, police and teachers used to confiscate the folding afro combs from Black people because they viewed the combs as potential weapons."

"But, Granny Mary, I've seen afro combs before, but they didn't look weapons, or the other ones you described."

Granny Mary smiled and said, "That's correct. Today, there are many different types of afro combs, and they are used to comb the hair, to adorn or decorate the hair, and make political statements. The afro combs in the hair function like the beautiful jewelry and ornaments that were put on geles to skirt restrictive Tignon laws of 1786 and celebrate Black Hair."

Penny raised her right hand, excitedly trying to interject into Granny Mary's exposition. As soon as Granny Mary paused, Penny said, "Granny Mary, some of the big boys that go to the Multilateral School put their afro combs in their hair after they leave school. And then they walk and bounce like they're cool dudes."

Granny Mary burst into uproarious laughter, and chimed in, "Yes, I know who you're talking about. One of the young men is Mr. Benjamin's last boy. He's a real character! When I was younger, schoolboys kept their afro combs in their back pockets or someplace where it was visible to the whole world, even though they risked being arrested. Today, many Black people are wearing afros again. They wear afros to show pride in their African heritage, to look attractive, to reject European standards of good hair and beauty, and to have healthy hair that is not damaged by processing. Some famous people who have worn afros include musicians, like the late Prince, Erykah Badu, Maxwell, Lenny Kravitz, Lauryn Hill, and Questlove who often wears an afro comb in his hair. However, one of the most popular people who wears an afro is American football player Colin Kaepernick. He is a talented quarterback that played in the National Football League (NFL) for the San Francisco 49ers and the Denver Broncos. In the summer of 2016, Colin began kneeling during the playing of American National Anthem, instead of standing with his right hand over his heart. Some people were upset with Colin because they said his actions were disrespectful to the American flag and American servicemen and servicewomen. However, Colin kept kneeling in protest because he wanted justice for the many unarmed Black people who were killed by police. Other athletes and people all over the world showed support for the cause by kneeling like Colin. Colin's kneeling during the anthem was very striking, but so was his big beautiful afro."

Penny seemed overwhelmed by the information. Clearly impressed, she looked at Granny Mary and said, "Wow! That is amazing! Did you also have an afro when you were young, Granny Mary?"

Granny Mary laughed and nodded. "My sweet girl, in my day I had a thick head of hair and tried every conceivable hairstyle. Now I am old, and my hair is *nyampy-nyampy* (patchy), so I wear my wigs and head-ties. I leave the fancy styles for young people."

Granny Mary turned the page and Penny exclaimed, "Look, Granny Mary, she has an afro, just like Colin."

Figure 10

"Indeed," Granny Mary began. "Long before Colin came along, Black people wore afros to look beautiful and show pride in their African heritage. For example, Angela Davis, Jesse Jackson, Huey P. Newton, and many other civil rights and political activists wore afros. Musicians, such as the Jackson 5, Sly & the Family Stone, and many performers on the television shows like *Soul Train*, also wore afros. The afro hairstyle was also seen in Blaxploitation films like *Coffy, Foxy Brown*, and *Shaft*. When we were younger, many of us wore afros and dashikis, especially in the 1970s, during the Black Power Movement."

Dreadlocks or Natty Dread

Figure 11

Granny Mary turned the page, pointed to a photo and said, "See this? Eclectic hair is sometimes locked?"

"Oooh! Bob Marley!" Penny shouted. "His hair is fat!"

Granny Mary smiled and nodded approvingly. "See how his hair seems to be matted, into large, thick, rope-like bands? He has dreadlocks or natty dreads. Bob Marley is a legendary musician, known for popularizing reggae music. He was born in Jamaica. When he was alive, he kept his hair in dreadlocks, because he was a Rasta."

"Oh, like Mr. Norris from Wallaba Street," Penny added.

"Yes, indeed!" Granny Mary responded. "Rasta or Rastafari is a religion that began in Jamaica and the Caribbean, and later spread to the rest of the world. The term Rastafari comes from Ras Tafar I Makonen, the pre-coronation name of Haile Selassie, Emperor of Ethiopia from 1930-1974. Rastas believe that Haile Selassie is the Messiah, so they worship him. Rastafari has many other beliefs, but dreadlocks or natty dread is one of the most visible symbols of their identity."

"Granny Mary, what other beliefs do Rastas have?" Penny asked.

"Well they do not eat meat or drink alcohol, and many smoke marijuana (an herb) for meditation," Granny Mary explained. "Rastas often pattern their lives after Samson, the character in the Bible, who was known as the strongest man. Samson made a Nazarite vow to God, which prevented him from drinking wine, eating certain things, and cutting his hair. In fact, many Rastas believe that if they cut their hair, they will lose their strength, just like Sampson. Their hair is also matted because they do not comb it."

"But, Granny Mary," Penny chimed in, "Ms. Brenda has locs but her hair doesn't look like dreadlocks."

Granny Mary nodded, "Yes, dear. Nowadays, many people lock their hair into smaller, more organized micro-locs, but they are not necessarily Rastas. See the photos lettered "A" and "B"? They have micro dreads or micro locs. To create micro-locs, some people use gels, wax, or other sticky substances, and spin the hair until it is matted into itself, just like they do to create natty dread. Other people use a special needle to interlock or knit their hair. When women wear micro locs, we call them sister-locs, and when men wear them, we call them mister-locs." Granny Mary laughs. "Like I said, sister-locs and mister-locs are not necessarily connected to a specific religion."

Micro Dreads: sister locs and mister locs

Figure 12

Penny shoots her hand into the air like a rocket, and Granny Mary stopped speaking. "Granny Mary, what is interlock. How do people interlock the hair?"

Granny Mary paused for a minute before beginning to speak. "Well, my dear, interlocking is like knitting. Whenever new hair grows out beneath the locs, a special needle is used to 'knit' the hair to use up the new growth, to lock it, and make the hair look neat. Understood?"

Penny smiles. "Understood!"

"Let's see what else we have here," Granny Mary says, as she turns the page and looks at a photo quizzingly. "Not this one. Let's keep the discussion on natural eclectic hair. Here we go!"

Individual Plaits (Braids)

Figure 13

"Braids!" Penny exclaimed. "Mommy makes my hair like this for school."

"Correct!" Granny Mary said. "In my day, we used to call them plaits (pronounced platts). To plait or braid the hair, you take three strands of hair and interlock them by taking the outer strands and crossing them over the middle strand, one side at a time, and alternating hands. Each time an outer strand crosses over the middle strand, that strand becomes the new middle strand. You have to keep crossing the middle strand by alternating the hands, until you get to the end of the hair."

"But Granny Mary, Mrs. Ben's grandson has braids and he's not even a girl!" Penny interjected."

"That's a good observation," Granny Mary replied. "Yes, sometimes boys and men wear plaits or braids for many different reasons. For instance, some people believe that if you cut a boy's hair before he turns one year old, he will never learn to speak. That's one of the many reasons that little boys in our community have plaits, free or 'wild' hair, and locs."

"Wow," I never knew that," Penny replied.

Granny Mary nodded, then continued, "On different note, schoolchildren in Guyana and the Caribbean often wear single plaits because school policies prevent them from wearing fancy hairstyles to school. When I was in primary school, I wore single plaits all the time. I did not wear other hairstyles until I started high school."

Penny chimed in, "Oh, yes, one day, Mrs. Griffith sent Beverly home because she came to school with the fancy hairstyle she wore to her brother's wedding. Mrs. Griffith shouted and said, "Beverly, go home and get rid of all that meh-cheh meh-cheh on top of your head." Penny laughed so hard her body shook.

Granny Mary joined Penny in laugher. She then returned her gaze to the album. "That's an interesting story. Well, sometimes, adults also plait their hair to get a meh-cheh meh-cheh hairstyle. You see, when the plaits are unraveled or loosed out, they leave the hair crinkled or wavy. So, some people wear the unraveled hair as a new hairstyle. Do you remember Debbie with the free hair?"

"Yes," said Penny.

"Well," Granny Mary explained, "she plaits her hair and unravels it to get the free or wild hairstyle she usually wears."

"Granny Mary, can you do my hair like that?" Penny asked.

Granny Mary chuckled. "You kinda had that hairstyle when you came over earlier today, thanks to Trevor."

Granny Mary smiled, but Penny pouted a little, still thinking about her nemesis Trevor.

"Now let's talk about a different kind of braids," Granny Mary said as she turned the page.

Regular Cornrows/Dutch Cornrows/Reverse French Braid/Outside Cornrows

Figure 14

"Granny Mary, I have had these before!" Penny exclaimed.

"Me too!" Granny Mary replied. "When I was young, we used to call them canerows, but today, y'all call them cornrows. Our ancestors have been braiding their hair for centuries and had different names for the types of braiding we do today."

"I like it when mommy braids my hair really fine (small), because then it doesn't get fuzzy when I play with my friends," Penny commented.

"Very true," Granny Mary said. "But let's continue our cornrow talk. Cornrows are made by braiding the hair towards the scalp in a sort of continuous motion. The first style is called Dutch braids, pineapple braids, and inverted or reverse French braids. However, in Guyana, we call it regular cornrows or outside cornrows. You braid regular cornrows by dipping your fingers outwards and under. You can braid both cornrows and single plaits in the regular or Dutch style."

Granny Mary turned the page, but before she could speak, Penny shouted, "But the first, Dutch cornrows don't look like the second one."

'Hassa-back'/French Cornrows

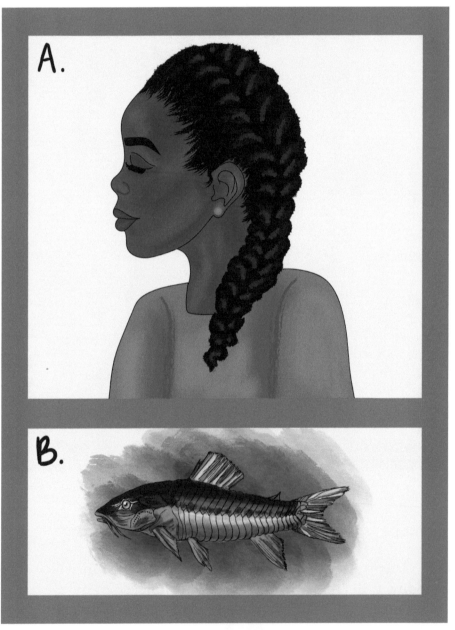

Figure 15

Granny Mary nodded her head in agreement and continued, "Well, they are both cornrows, but they are made differently. The cornrow in **Figure 15A** is called a French Braid or Oklahoma plait. To make this style, you move your fingers inward and under in one continuous motion. In Guyana, we call the French cornrows 'hassa-back,' because they resemble the body of the hassa fish (**Fig. 15B**). You see, hassa is a kind of catfish that lives in fresh water. So, you can find hassa in Guyana and other countries in South America, where there are bodies of fresh water. Hassa live in the muddy bottoms of trenches, rivers, swamps, and streams, and often swim in large groups called 'schools.'"

"Granny Mary, did you see hassa when you were growing up?" Penny asked.

Granny Mary responded, "Of course. When we were young, we used to haul the trench in Sandvoort Village to catch hassa. To haul the trench, we would drag a fishing net along the bottom of the trench, while walking along the sides of the trench or rowing a canoe. Sometimes my friends and I would haul the trench by holding the opposite ends of an old curtain or bedsheet and dragging it along the bottom of the trench. In order to catch the most fish, we would form two teams that begin at opposite ends of the trench, and move towards each other, to the center of the trench. When we took our catch home, our mothers would make fried fish, curried hassa, and other delicious meals. Those were good times, honey!"

Clearly flabbergasted, Penny exclaimed, "Wow! That's amazing! I can't believe how much the hassa fish looks like the hassa-back cornrow!"

"Indeed," said Granny Mary. "And there's so much more natural eclectic hair to discuss."

Senegalese Twists

Granny Mary turned the page and said, "Now, let's talk about *twists*!"

Figure 16

Looking up at Penny, Granny Mary said, "See her head? These are called Senegalese twists. The Republic of Senegal is located in West Africa and has many different ethnic groups. There are also many different languages spoken in Senegal, including Wolof, Arabic, and French. Senegalese twists are created by taking two bundles of hair and twisting them around each other in the opposite direction. You start from the root or scalp of the hair and twists until you get to the end of the hair. The beautiful and talented American actress, Kerry Washington, is one of the famous Black women who have worn Senegalese twists."

"That's pretty," Penny said, "and easy too. I can do that by myself. You know, Granny Mary, sometimes I take out some of my hair at the sides of my head and make twists. I can do this all over my own head."

"You're right!" Granny Mary said. "I think you can easily make this hairstyle."

Bantu Knots

Figure 17

As soon as Granny Mary turned the page, Penny exclaimed, "That's A-M-A-Z-I-N-G! Her hairstyle looks like a bunch of tiny coconut buns or cinnamon rolls." Penny laughs uncontrollably while staring at the photo.

Granny Mary started laughing too. After a short while, she said to Penny, "You are too funny! These are called *bantu knots*. You make bantu knots by taking a bundle of hair and twisting it around itself. Then, you circle the twisted hair around the base of the hair, as if you're stacking tires. A person can wear bantu knots as a hairstyle or unravel it to create a curly, free hairstyle, like you do with unraveled braids."

"I wonder who came up with this hairstyle," Penny said.

Granny Mary repositioned herself in her chair and began, "I think, based on the name, this hairstyle came from the Bantu-speaking people of Central and Southern Africa. The Bantu people belong to more than four hundred ethnic groups and speak more than five hundred different Bantu languages. Today, many people know about Bantu knots largely because of migration and the media. One of the most famous people who wore Bantu knots is Rihanna, the Barbados-born singer, actress, and businesswoman."

Threaded hair

Figure 18

Granny Mary turned the page, and Penny shouted, "Woa! Ropes! Sticks! What are those?!!"

Granny Mary threw her head backwards and laughed heartily, as she readied herself to deliver another mini lecture. "No, child, this is threaded hair. Threading is a traditional African practice. To create this hairstyle, you part the hair into sections, as if you're going to plait it, then you use thread or sturdy yarn to tightly wrap each section of the hair. The thread must be strong, or it will break. Sometimes people use yarn, instead of thread, in order to wrap the hair in less time. Threading keeps the hair neat for a long time. It also helps the hair grow faster, since the hair is not being disturbed by combing or processing. Many ethnic groups in Ghana, Nigeria, and other countries in Sub-Saharan Africa (below the Sahara Desert) practice hair threading. They also have different names for the threaded hairstyle. The Igbos (pronounced Ee-bows) of Nigeria called threading *isi owu*. *Isi* (ee-see) means 'head' and *owu* (oh-woo) means 'cotton' or 'thread.' So, *isi owu* literally means threaded head, referring to the hairstyle. Among the Yoruba people of Nigeria, threaded hair was referred to as *irun kiko*. In Yoruba, *irun* means 'hair' and *kiko* means 'gather'; so *irun kiko* literally means 'gathered hair' or 'threaded hair.' The Yoruba people also refer to threaded hair that points straight outwards as *onigi*, which literally means 'sticks.' So, your observations are correct."

"Do people still wear threaded hair in Africa?" Penny asked.

"Of course," said Granny. "But some of the styles have changed, and now there are many newer styles that resemble the older ones."

"How did threaded hairstyles change, Granny Mary?" Penny asked.

Granny Mary smiled and said, "Girl, that's a conversation for a whole day."

Penny interjected, "Well, Granny Mary, you can make it shorter than a day."

Granny Mary chuckled. "Of course, I can try. Well, in pre-colonial Africa, before Europeans invaded the continent, hair was threaded with natural materials like raffia fronds (**Fig. 19B**), which are leaves from the raffia palm (**Fig. 19A**). Africans rubbed or beat the green raffia palm frond until it revealed the white or transparent strips of material on the inside. Those strips were then dried and used to wrap the hair. Sometimes, women dyed the dried raffia strips with natural dyes from fruits, vegetables, and plants. So, the strips used to wrap the hair were of different colours. For instance, the Igbos dyed the strips black by using the juice from a fruit called *uri*. When Europeans began trading wool with Africans, women began threading the hair with wool instead of raffia frond and other natural materials. This is partly because it took less time to thread the hair with wool than with raffia. The hairstyle also lasted longer because the wool was stronger than raffia fronds."

"This is so intriguing," Penny mused. "And the raffia tree is big and beautiful!"

Granny Mary chimed in, "And important too! You see, the raffia palm fronds are also used to make the skirts and other parts of masquerades. Masquerades are like grand performances, ceremonies, or plays that tell stories about the people who participate in them. Masquerade performers often wear masks and other types of costumes that hide their identities. Masquerades can be entertaining, but they also tell about history, culture, spiritual beliefs, and many other aspects of a society."

Figure 19

Just as Penny was about to raise her hand, Granny Mary, interjected and said, "Oh, another thing, the raffia palm tree also produces delicious palm wine. Africans drink palm wine every day to quench their thirst. They also drink palm wine during important events like weddings, naming ceremonies for babies, and funerals. On special occasions, Africans also offer libations (offerings) to their ancestors and deities, by pouring some palm wine onto the ground."

"So, from the same palm tree they get palm fronds (leaves) and palm wine?" Penny asked.

"Well, sort of," Granny Mary said. "There are different kinds of palm trees in Africa and they all have fronds or leaves that were used to thread the hair and in masquerades. However, some palm trees produce palm wine only, and some produce the nuts from which palm oil is extracted as well as a little palm wine. You know, even the coconut trees we have in our compound are types of palm trees."

"So, you're saying palm fronds were used for masquerades and to thread the hair?" Penny queried.

"Exactly," Granny Mary said. "Early Christian missionaries to Africa rejected certain African hairstyles, partly because those hairstyles were styled with the same raffia palm used in masquerades. Some Christian missionaries also wanted Africans to reject certain African hairstyles because those hairstyles, like masquerades, were connected to African spirituality. Moreover, they viewed African hairstyles, and African things in general, as strange because they were different, and not European..."

"But we have masquerades in Guyana too," Penny interjected.

"Yes, we do," Granny Mary replied. "You know, our Guyanese masquerades were derived from African masquerades. When we were young, masquerades would visit our homes around at Christmas time. The masquerade consisted of about seven men, who wore brightly coloured costumes, flounced (a type of dance), beat drums, and played wooden flutes and other percussive instruments. At the end of their performance, people gave them money, black cake (dark fruit cake with rum), ginger beer, pepperpot and bread, and other types of Guyanese foods. I used to be so afraid of the masquerade!"

"I have a question, Granny Mary," Penny said. "Do people from other parts of the world still wear threaded hair?"

"Of course," Granny Mary replied. "Chidinma, the popular Nigerian singer, sometimes wears beautifully threaded hair. Also, when I was young, many parents in Sandvoort Village, Victoria, Buxton, and other former African villages in Guyana used to thread their daughters' hair. My mother threaded my hair many times for weddings and other special occasions. I remember it being a long and painful process, but the hairstyles were always beautiful."

Granny Mary paused for a minute, then said, "Threading has many functions, but we'll talk about some of those later."

Penny calmly reached over the table and turned the page (Go back to Figure 18). "Granny Mary, this is the same lady with threaded hair that looks like sticks, *onigi*!"

"Yes, it is!" Granny Mary replied. "I included it because threading is a form of hair processing, which I'll tell you more about later. When the hair is wrapped in yarn or threaded, it puts pressure on each strand of hair. After a while, the stress or tension on the hair causes the tight curls of woolly hair to relax and straighten themselves out. When the yarn is later removed from the hair, the hair looks straighter than the natural tightly curled hair. So, even though the hair is still natural, it looks like it has been processed and changed."

Granny Mary turned the page and smiled, anticipating Penny's response.

Figure 20

Penny leaned her head way back and said exasperatedly, "Threading, agaaaain!"

Granny Mary explained, "I know you know what this hairstyle is, but threading lets the wearer look beautiful by letting them create an array of different hairstyles. Earlier, I showed you threaded hair that sticks outwards, but see how this style are curly and fancy? That's because the threaded hair can be easily bent, curled, and shaped into different designs. Some of the fancy hairstyles that are created with threaded hair look like baskets, crowns, pineapples, and other objects."

"So, anyone can make their threaded hair curly and fancy, right?" Penny asked.

"Well, yes," Granny Mary said. "But different women design their threaded hair for different reasons. For instance, African women style their threaded hair in certain ways to insult each other."

"But how do they know when it's an insult?" Penny asked.

Granny Mary explained, "Well, when people grow up in a culture, they learn how to behave, to communicate, and to understand unique things about that culture. We call that kind of learning 'enculturation.'"

Combination hairstyles

Figure 21

Granny Mary turns the page, and exclaimed, "Oh look! You're familiar with this hairstyle, right?"

"That's just a bunch of different stuff!" Penny replied.

Granny Mary smiled and said, "Yes, sometimes Black people wear a combination of different hairstyles. So, they might combine cornrows, puffs, twists, and other different styles. Combination hairstyles allow the hairstylist to showcase their creativity, and let the person wearing the hairstyle be extra fancy. The award-winning Nigerian author, Chimamanda Ngozi Adichie, often wears combination hairstyles that include puffs, cornrows, twists, and other designs in her natural hair."

"Are we donc, Granny Mary? Are those all the eclectic hair?" Penny asked anxiously.

"No, my dear." Granny Mary laughed. "You're not getting off that easily. We have more to talk about. Our hair is so amazing, we can't just stop here."

Penny smiled Granny Mary chuckled.

Chapter 3:

Processed Eclectic Hair

Granny Mary turned the page of the album and gave out a sigh. Then, she said, "Lovie, in this section, you will see some of the different ways that eclectic hair is processed. By 'processed,' I mean the natural texture and colour of the hair is changed by putting something *in* or *on* the hair."

Penny interjected, "Mommy has processed hair. She always goes to the hairdresser with puffy hair and comes back with it looking straight, flat, and shiny. I think she gets a perm."

Granny Mary laughed, and said, "Yes, I think she gets a perm, which we'll talk about more in a few minutes. You see, sweetie, Black people have always processed their hair, but today, they have different ways of doing so. Long before Europeans colonized Africa, Africans processed their hair using oils, yarns, and other substances and materials. However, during the colonial period and Slavery, Black people were made to feel ashamed for their hair texture, their methods of processing the hair, and their hairstyles. However, with the constant development of new technology, processing creams, and hair products, Black people around the world are finding new ways to transform their hair textures, colours, and styles. Today, Black people continue to process their hair for different reasons. For instance, some people process their hair to make it more 'manageable'; some process their hair to create certain styles; some process their hair because they think it makes them look beautiful; and sadly, some process their hair to look less Black or to reject their African heritage."

Relaxed hair: Perm

Granny Mary turned the page, but before she could say anything, Penny exclaimed, "She has a perm, Granny!"

Figure 22

"You're on a roll today, eh?" Granny Mary said laughing. "And, yes, she does. Black people sometimes process their hair using relaxers, also called perms. Relaxers are chemical creams or lotions that are added to Black hair to change its structure and appearance. The relaxer cream is applied to the base of the hair and left to 'cook' (work) for about fifteen minutes. The cream is then rinsed out completely. Certain chemicals in the relaxers, such as sodium hydroxide (known as NaOH or lye) and potassium hydroxide (KOH), break down the structure of woolly Black hair.

This causes the hair to stretch out or lay flat on the head and look longer than in its natural state. The hair has to be relaxed every 2-3 months in order to straighten new hair growth and make all the hair look straight."

Penny knew Granny Mary would give her more background information, so she chimed in, "Where did the relaxer come from?"

Granny Mary smiled approvingly and explained, "An African-American man named Garrett Augustus Morgan is credited with accidentally inventing the first hair straightening cream. Mr. Morgan owned a sewing machine shop and was trying to find a way to lubricate his sewing machine to prevent friction and stop it from creaking. So, he developed a cream and tested it on the fur of his neighbour's dog. The cream turned the dog's fur straight. Later, Mr. Morgan began to sell this cream to people who were Black and mixed race. He became so successful that he established G.A. Morgan Hair Refining Company. Today, there are many companies that produce different types of relaxers."

Penny furrowed her brow, leaned over the table, and looked at Granny Mary quizzingly, "But since the relaxer-perm was first used on machines and dogs, isn't it bad for human hair?"

"Well, yes," Granny Mary replied. "The relaxer can destroy the hair and burn the scalp, but many Black people say that once you begin relaxing the hair, it is difficult to stop, much like an addiction. In fact, many Black people refer to the relaxer cream as "creamy crack" because they see it as both dangerous and addictive."

"Did you get a relaxer too, Granny Mary?" Penny asked.

Granny Mary replied, "Of course! When I was about twenty years old, I took a vacation to London, England. Before I left Guyana, my Aunt Patty took me to the hairdresser, and I got a relaxer. She thought that hair that lays flat on the head would make me look cultured or sophisticated. However, I think the hairdresser left the cream in my hair too long because it burned my scalp and made some of my hair fall out. Well, my hair laid flat, but I ended up wearing a beret for most of the trip. It took months for my scalp to heal, and maybe a year before my hair grew back properly."

She quizzed further, "So, you didn't use relaxers after that?" "Of course, I did," Granny Mary replied, while chuckling. "I was a very vain person. Of course, I got more relaxers. I also used other types of creams."

"What other types of processing creams did you use, Granny Mary?" Penny asked.

Jheri curl

Figure 23

"Well, I used the jheri curl cream," Granny Mary began. "In the 1980s and 1990s, chemical creams that helped produce jheri curls were very popular. An American named Robert William Redding (known as Jheri Redding) created the jheri curl. In fact, the term 'jheri curl' came from Mr. Redding's nickname 'Jheri'. Mr. Redding was a chemist, a hairdresser, and an entrepreneur. In addition to the jheri curl, he also created hair conditioners, shampoos, and hair products with vitamins to nourish the hair."

"How do you get the hair to jheri curl," Penny quizzed further.

Providing her characteristically detailed response, Granny Mary began: "A jheri curl cream, just like the relaxer cream, is first applied to the base of the hair. The cream is left to sit or 'cook' for several minutes, so the chemicals in it can straighten the tight curls of woolly Black hair. After the relaxer cream is washed out of the hair, special conditioners and other chemicals are added to the straightened hair to make it create large curls or waves. To keep the jheri curls looking fresh, moisturizers and curl activator sprays must be added to the hair every day. So, the hair always looks shiny and feels oily and damp or wet. Jheri curls used to be so messy! Sometimes, people with jheri curls would leave greasy patches on pillows and the backs of the couches they sat in. Today, cosmetologists are finding newer ways to recreate the jheri curl look without all that greasy mess."

As soon as Granny Mary turned the page, Penny popped up from her chair and exclaimed, "That's Michael Jackson!"

Granny Mary laughed so loudly that wrinkles appeared in the corners of her eyes. "Yes, indeed," she said. "Michael Jackson was a legendary singer and dancer who began performing with his brothers in a group called 'The Jackson Five.' At the height of his career in the 1980s and 1990s, he wore jheri curls. In fact, in the photo on the cover of his *Thriller* album, he has jheri curls. Some other popular people who have worn jheri curls include singers Edmund Sylvers and Lionel Ritchie, rappers Ice Cube and Eazy-E, and actor Eriq La Salle who acted in the movie *Coming to America*."

"Wow, Granny Mary! You really know a LOT of things! By the way, are there other ways to process the hair?" Penny asked.

"Thanks, lovie," Granny Mary replied. "Well, sometimes Black people also use heat to straighten or process their hair. The heat relaxes the tight curls and make the hair straight, but it also damages the hair in the process."

Pressing comb and Hot Irons

Granny Mary turned the page to reveal four pictures.

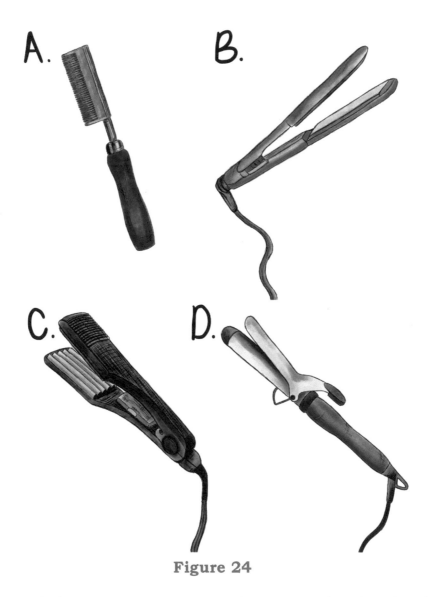

Figure 24

Unable to wait for Granny Mary to speak, Penny pointed to the picture labeled "A" and asked, "What is this?"

Granny Mary explained, "Well, Pen-Pen, this is a hot comb or pressing comb. It is used to straighten tightly curled woolly hair like ours. The metal comb is placed on the stove or some other heating source to make it hot, and then it is used to comb the hair. The heat stretches out the hair and makes it look longer and lay flat. When I was younger, I used to get my hair straightened with a pressing comb. I could hear the hair grease frying as the pressing comb passed through my hair. Many times, the hairdresser would accidentally burn my ears, scalp, or neck, and cause me so much pain." Granny Mary laughed and continued, "I think every woman who ever had her hair pressed, had the awful experience of being burned. Unlike relaxers and other creams, hair that is straightened with the pressing comb or other heat sources does not stay straight for a long time. Once it gets wet, it returns to its natural curly, woolly state."

"Wow!" Penny exclaimed.

Then, pointing to the picture labeled "D", Penny said, "I know the curling iron. Mommy has one of these!"

"Very good," Granny Mary said smiling. The instruments labeled 'B,' 'C' and 'D' are called hair irons or hair tongs. There are three main types of hair irons: the flat iron 'B,' the crimper 'C', and the curling iron 'D'. Each hair iron uses heat to process the hair to change its texture and style. It is said that in the 1870s, a French hairdresser named Marcel Grateau began using heated metals like the hot comb, to straighten the hair. However, it was not until 1909 when Isaac K. Shero patented the first flat iron. In earlier times, hot irons were heated on stoves and open fires, but nowadays, ceramic and electrical hot irons allow the user to control the heat, so as not to burn the hair."

"So, the picture labeled 'B' is the flat iron?" Penny asked.

"Yes," Granny Mary said. She continued, "The flat iron is generally used to straighten the hair. The flat iron looks like a clamp with two flat metal plates on each clamp. The plates heat up when the flat iron is plugged into an electric source. The hair is placed between the two clamps at the root of the hair and closed. The clamp is then pulled along the length of the hair, from the root to the tip. The heat straightens the hair by relaxing the tight curls of the natural woolly Black hair."

Penny looked at Granny Mary's head-tie and said, "So, I'm guessing you have used a flat iron too, right?"

Granny Mary began laughing raucously, and said, "Of course! Wanna hear a funny story? In the 1960s we used to use the clothes iron to straighten our hair. We would lay our hair flat on an object that could not burn, like an enamel plate or a piece of aluminum, and then, run the iron along the length of the hair. Some of my friends who had longer hair, used to lay their hair on an ironing board or a flat surface, and press it like clothes. Good grief, that was so dangerous, and we were nuts to do that!"

"What about the picture labeled "C"? Penny asked. "It looks like the flat iron."

Granny Mary said, "Oh, yes it does! It is called a crimping iron or a crimper. Just like the flat iron, it is a clamp with metal plates. However, the plates on the crimper are wavy with crests (peaks) and troughs (indentations). The modern-day crimper was invented in 1972 by Geri Cusenza, the founder of Sebastian, a hair products company. It is said that Geri Cusenza created the crimper to design the hair of legendary American singer Barbara Streisand."

"Wow!" Penny exclaimed.

Granny Mary continued, "To crimp the hair, the crimper is placed over a section of the hair and the clamp is closed firmly. When the clamp is opened, the hair takes the design of the crests and troughs on the metal plate and looks wavy. To crimp the entire length of the hair, the process must be repeated several times, beginning at the scalp, and moving towards the end of the hair. Because it changes the texture and shape of the hair at the same time, the crimper can be used on natural hair as well as hair that is already processed. It straightens natural hair while crimping it, and crimps already straightened hair."

"Now, onto the curling iron, labeled 'D'," Granny Mary said. "You already told me that your mommy has one."

"Yes, she does," Penny replied. "She curled my hair with it for Easter Sunday last year."

"Good! So, you already know how it is used, right?" Granny Mary quipped.

"Yes, I do!" Penny said. "You start close to the scalp, and you put the hair between the barrel and the clamp of the curling iron. Then, you keep turning the curling iron, so the hair wraps around it as you move it towards the end of the hair."

Clearly impressed with Penny's detailed answer, Granny Mary laughed and said, "Very good, smarty pants! But you know, the curling iron we use is generally cylindrical with a long barrel-like body. It is made of metal, Teflon, or some other heat-resistant material. You can curl the natural hair by spinning it around the curling iron in a spiral fashion. However, you can also straighten the hair by clamping it and running it along the length of the hair. The curling iron can be used on natural hair as well as hair that is already processed and straightened."

Blow dryer, Bonnet Dryer, and Cap (hood) Dryer

Granny Mary turned the page to reveal three more photos. "Look at this!" she said to Penny.

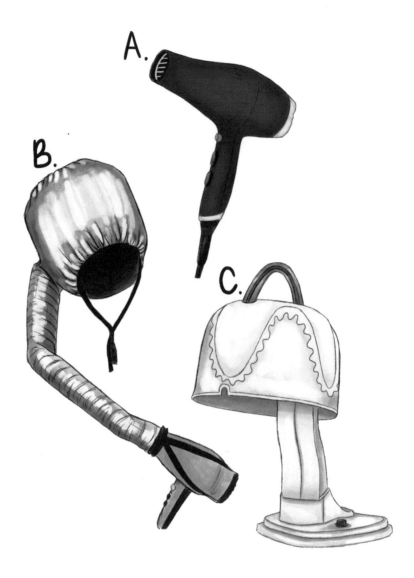

Figure 25

In her characteristic manner, Penny stuck her hand into the air to get Granny Mary's attention. Before Granny Mary could respond, Penny shouted, "The first one **(A)** is a blow dryer, for drying wet hair."

"Yes, but not only for drying hair, my dear," Granny Mary added. "It is also used to straighten the hair. Nowadays, they even make special kinds of hairdryers to straighten the hair. To straighten the hair with a blow dryer, you need a comb in one hand and the blow dryer in the other. While combing through the hair with one hand, you move the blow dryer along the hair, close to the comb, with the other. The blow dryer makes the hair look just as straight as other heating methods or chemical creams."

Granny Mary took a deep breath, sipped some tea, and continued, "In my day, we used a bonnet dryer **(B)**, which fit on the head like a shower cap and had a hose through which the air was blown onto the head. We would wash our hair, put rollers in it while it was still wet, and then, sit under the bonnet dryer. When the hair dried, it took the shape of the hair roller. We also used to put rollers in our dry hair and sit under the dryer, so that the heat from the bonnet dryer could curl our hair. We also used a cap or hood dryer **(C),** which we will talk about in a minute."

"Ok, Granny Mary. Question…" Penny said.

"Yes, I know you want to know where dryers came from," Granny Mary interjected. "Well, my dear, the hair dryer was invented in 1890 by Alexander Godefroy, a French hairstylist. That earlier version of the hairdryer had a bonnet that was connected to a gas stove through its chimney pipe. However, it was not until 1911 that that first hair dryer was patented in the United States by an Armenian American named Gabriel Kazanjian."

Granny Mary sipped some more tea and inhaled deeply. After a few seconds, she continued, "By the 1920s, handheld hairdryers, like the one in box "A", were marketed to the public and became popular. However, during the earlier years, handheld hairdryers often overheated, causing burns and electrocution. With technological advances, handheld dryers and bonnet dryers became safer to use."

"What about the hood dryer, Granny Mary?" Penny asked.

Granny Mary responded, "Well, the cap or hood dryer was introduced to society in the 1950s. It is like the bonnet dryer, but the cap or hood is like a hardhat that sits above the head and blows hot hair, which evaporates moisture from the hair."

Then, as if she forgot something, Granny Mary quickly raised her index finger to her lips and said, "Today, there are also electric hairbrushes, and many other hair tools that use heat to straighten the hair, but we can never cover them all."

Chapter 4:

Eclectic Hair with Additions

"What else you got, granny?" Penny asked.

Granny Mary smiled and replied, "More eclectic hair. We'll look at eclectic hair that has additions or extensions. You know, sometimes, eclectic hair *is* extra because it *has* extra. See this?!"

Wigs

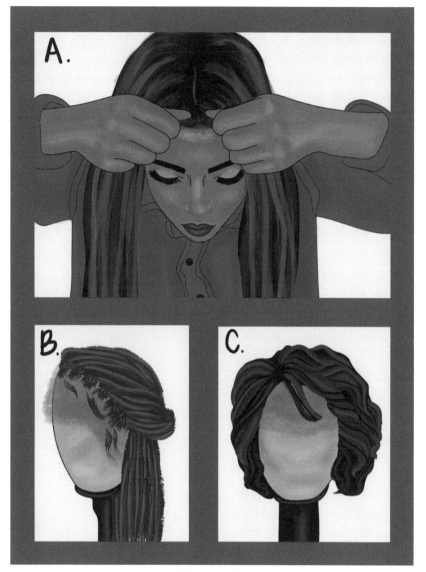

Figure 26

"Those are wigs!" Penny shouted excitedly, as she points to a page with three pictures. "My teacher, Mrs. Marks, has a wig like that."

Through her laughter, Granny Mary said, "Yes. Those are wigs. Before the 1600s, they were called periwigs." Granny Mary continued, "In ancient Egypt, people generally kept their heads bald or their hair extremely low. So, wigs helped to protect the head from the sun. To keep the wig firmly on the head and prevent it from falling off, they used sticky substances like beeswax or resin. Other ancient cultures—such as Greeks, Jews, and Romans—also used wigs for different reasons. Back then, wigs were made of human hair, as well as from the hair of horses and goats. Later on, wigs were worn to hide hair loss, to protect the hair from lice, to highlight social status (like royalty or military), to indicate profession (such as barrister, judge, and politician), for religious observance (as with some orthodox Jewish women), and for many other reasons. Throughout history, the style and function of wigs have changed drastically."

"How do they get the hair to stick together like that to go on the head," Penny asked.

Granny Mary laughed and said, "I can read your mind, sweetie. Well, wigs are generally made by affixing or attaching natural or synthetic (fake) hair to a soft, cap-like base. Because the base is kind of soft, a person can easily pull the wig onto the head. A lot of women braid their natural hair into cornrows before putting on a wig. Some individuals also put on a stocking cap over their natural hair before putting on a wig. Braiding or covering the natural hair first, helps the wig to fit neatly on the head."

Staring intently at the photo, Penny asked, "Who's that woman, Granny Mary?"

"This is a photo of my mother, your great-grandmother," Granny Mary replied. "Back in the day, she and many other women wore wigs to cover their natural hair, especially when they began to lose their hair, or when the hair turned grey. The wig was an instant hairstyle. So, many older women wore wigs when they got dressed up for church or special events. Sometimes they even wore wigs at home to look presentable when entertaining guests. A lot of the wigs that older people wore back then had shorter hair."

Granny Mary turned her gaze towards the teapot, and said to Penny, "Here have some more tea, pumpkin." She poured the tea for Penny, then said, "Now let's continue."

"Nowadays, there are so many different types of wigs," Granny Mary continued. "Some wigs are short, some are long, some are curly, some are afros, some have braided hair, some have locs, some have Bantu knots, and many other eclectic styles. Wigs are also made with diverse colours. Moreover, not only old people wear wigs. A lot of young people wear wigs made from human hair that comes from Brazil, India, and other parts of the world. Some people even buy the materials and make their own wigs. Wig creators are also making wigs that look more like real hair that grows out of the scalp. See this woman? She is wearing a long, wavy wig that is made of Brazilian hair."

"Do you have a wig, Granny Mary?" Penny asked.

"Oh, yes!" Granny Mary said. "I have three wigs. I have a special wig that I only wear to church, weddings, and important events. Then, I have my good wig I sometimes wear to parties, meetings, and not-so-special events. And my third wig is my house wig that I just slap on my head when friends come to visit. I'm wearing my house wig right now under my head-tie. I will show you the other two once we're done going through these photos."

Granny Mary turned the page and said, "Here's another interesting photo!"

Box Braids

Figure 27

Clearly exasperated, Penny said, "Braids again?!!"

"Yes, braids again," Granny Mary replied as she readied herself to deliver another exposition. "You see, sweat pea, these are braids, but they are different than the ones I showed you before. These braids have extensions. To create this style, you take synthetic or natural hair and braid strands into your own natural hair. The extensions give the hair a sort of 'boxy' appearance, hence the term 'box braids.' You create box braids like you create single braids or plaits, but you have to braid hair extensions into the hair before you get to the end of the braid. Some people insert the extensions at the beginning of the braid, but others add them to the middle or some other part of the braid. Depending on how small the braids are, plaiting box braids can take a couple of hours to an entire day to compete. In pre-colonial Africa, women braided different materials into the hair. Sometimes, they added palm fronds (leaves), bamboo strips, grass, and other materials into the hair for different reasons. Today, women use human hair or synthetic hair to create box braids. When the hair extensions are made of synthetic (fake) materials that are not human hair, you have to burn the ends with a cigarette lighter to prevent it from unraveling."

"Wouldn't burning the hair make it catch afire?" Penny asked.

"No, not if you're careful," Granny Mary replied. "You have to quickly put out the tiny flame using your thumb and index finger. The fire melts the ends of the synthetic hair like plastic and causes them to fuse together. This prevents the ends of the hair from unraveling. You don't have to do this with the ends of natural hair, since it tends to knit itself together naturally."

"Granny Mary, how do you know if someone has natural plaits or box braids?" Penny asked.

Granny Mary said, "Sometimes, if you look at the root of the hair, you can see where the extensions begin. But this doesn't work every time because some people may choose to start the braid with the natural hair and then insert extensions in the middle of the plait. The best way to tell if someone has box braids is by looking at the length of the braid. Braided hair with extensions tends to be longer than average black hair. Box braids can even be two feet or more in length. You can also spot box braids by looking at the texture of the hair. Two popular Black women who wear box braids are Beyonce, the American singer and actress, and Letitia Wright, the Guyana-born actress who acted as Shuri in the Black Panther movie. Some people also braid yarn, ribbons, and other objects into the hair as colourful extensions. Most Black people can identify box braids without even touching it. You learn these things by being in the Black community and watching people create these hairstyles. Sometimes, if you spend time at the barber shop or hair salon, you might get to see how some of these hairstyles are created."

Granny Mary paused, then began speaking again. "Remember we talked about locs? Well, some people also add locs by sewing it on or braiding it into their natural. After a while, the locs extensions knits itself to the woolly Black hair. So, it's a bit harder to tell the difference between the natural hair and the locs extension."

Penny popped up once again and excitedly turned the page. She asked, "Granny Mary, does she have a relaxer, a press, or, maybe, it's flat-ironed hair?"

Weaves

Figure 28

Smiling warmly, Granny Mary replied, "I'm impressed you remembered all those types of eclectic hair. She is actually wearing a weave."

"Is that like a wig?" Penny asked.

Granny Mary said, "Well, it's an addition, but it's done differently. She continued, "Wigs are added onto the head while weaves are added to the hair itself. Sometimes it's difficult to tell what kind of hair addition a person has. If, for example, a weave is done neatly and intricately, or a wig is made with human hair and designed to look like the human scalp, you might not know. In those cases, only the head that wears it knows."

Granny Mary chuckled, and continued, "Weaves became popular in the 1950s, during the disco period, when people wore big hair or long hair additions. There are different kinds of weaves and they are added to the hair in different ways. Weaves are often added to the natural hair for length or volume. Pinchbraid extensions are made by tying individual locs of hair to a person's hair using a strong thread. Pinchbraids can also be made by braiding human or synthetic hair extensions onto the hair; after about an inch of braiding, a strand of the hair is used to create a knot that ties off the braid to prevent it from unraveling. The rest of the hair is left to flow freely, while the braided base is hidden."

"Oh yes," Granny Mary said, slightly closing her eyes. "Some weave extensions are also affixed to the hair using clips. The clips of the weave are sewn into the hair and then used to clip or hold individual locs or clumps of hair additions. The clip-in weave is easy to add and remove, so more people are choosing to wear it. Some weaves also have tiny combs affixed to the top pane. The combs are stuck into the base of the hair or cornrow and can be easily removed when needed."

"What kind of weave did you wear, Granny Mary?" Penny asked.

Granny Mary responded, "Well, one of the most popular kinds of weave looks like a panel of hair, suspended on a cord. That's the kind of weave I tried. It's as if individual strands of hair are sewn into a cord, so they hang like clothes on a line. To attach the weave, the hair is parted, and the cord-like part is glued to the base of the hair. Sometimes, the hair is first braided into cornrows that create 'tracks,' and then the cord-like base of the weave is sewn into the cornrows (**Fig. 25A**). Whatever method is used, the goal is to make sure that you hide the tracks (**Fig. 25B**). The tracks are the parts or sections where the weave is connected to a person's hair."

Interesting Additions: Otjize paste

Figure 29

Granny Mary turned the page and pointed to the picture labeled "A". She said, "Oh look! Here is an interesting addition we don't see in Guyana."

"Wait, does this woman have mud in her hair?" Penny asked in disbelief.

Laughing loudly and uncontrollably, Granny Mary shook her head vigorously and said, "Yes, she does! This woman belongs to the Himba (OvaHimba) ethnic group in Africa. The Himba people live in northern Namibia and Southern Angola on the continent of Africa. The Himba are pastoralists; they herd livestock like cattle and goats for food and other resources. Himba women cover their hair and skin with the *otjize* paste, which is a mixture of butterfat and the reddish *ochre* (a type of clay). The perfumed resin of the *omuzumba* plant is also added to the mixture to give it a sweet smell. The *Otjiize* paste gives the hair and skin a reddish-orange appearance. The Himba cover their skin with this mixture to protect them from extremely hot, dry weather, insect bites, and limited water supply. Himba women have many *otjize* plaits, and married Himba women wear special adornments or decorations in their hair to indicate that they are married."

Granny Mary points to the picture labeled "B" and said, "See this man? He is also Himba, but unlike the women, Himba men usually have a single hassa-back cornrow (French cornrow) in the center of their heads."

"Granny, did YOU ever use *otjize* paste in your hair?" Penny asked.

Chuckling, Granny Mary replied, "Well, lovie, you've found the only hairstyle your granny has never tried! But hey, it's never too late. Once there's life there's hope."

Penny joined Granny Mary and they laughed at the possibility of Granny Mary trying *otjize* paste in her old age.

After a little while, Penny redirected her focus to the album and asked, "What other kinds of additions do Black people add to their hair?"

Granny Mary, thought for a while, then said, "Remember, I told about how the Himba (OvaHimba) of Angola and Namibia put *otjize* paste in their hair?"

Figure 30

"Yes, you did," Penny responded.

"Well," Granny Mary continued, "Among the Maasai people of central and southern Kenya and northern Tanzania, the men have long hair, and they put interesting things in it. You see, the Maasai men pass through different stages or grades of manhood, which require them to shave their heads, and perform rituals called *rites of passage*. Between each grade, they grow out their hair, which is cut off at least twice in their lifetime. However, when a Maasai man completes the warrior grade and becomes a warrior, he grows his hair. Maasai warriors braid their hair into micro braids, and add animal fat, clay, and other substances to the hair to style it, and give it the reddish-orange *ochre* colour, like the Himba women.

The hair is styled by knitting the braids together using thread made of cotton or wool. The men also add colourful beads and other adornments to the hair to make it look attractive. Massai warriors view their long hair as a symbol of beauty and strength, much like the mane of the lion, 'king of the jungle.' Because their hair is such an important symbol of their identity, Maasai warriors spend hours styling their hair."

Chapter 5

Baldness: Eclectic Hair is No Hair

Figure 31

As soon as Granny Mary turned the page, Penny stated, "Ok, he's just bald. How is this eclectic?"

"He's bald alright. But bald is also a style," Granny Mary said, clearly amused by her own comment. "Some people have bald heads because of nature. As they get older, they lose their hair and may become completely bald. Some people may lose patches of hair and then decide to cut off the rest of it to make it even. This man resembles the late John Lewis. He was an American congressman from the state of Georgia and great Civil Rights activist who fought for Black people to have equal rights as everyone else. When he was young, he had a lot of hair, but when he got older, he had a bald head. I don't know if he cut off his hair, went completely bald, or a result of both."

"Ooh ooh, Granny Mary," Penny interjected. "Do you remember, the little old lady who made cookup rice for us when we visited Buxton Village? She was bald."

Granny Mary nodded in agreement, and said, "Correct! That was Ms. Sylvester. When she was young, she had a thick head of hair that she straightened with a pressing comb every weekend, but now, she is completely bald because she cut off her hair. She no longer wanted the stress of washing, combing, and styling her hair every day. So, you see, sometimes, a bald head is a hair choice men and women make for different reasons."

Jokingly, Penny said, "Reasons, reasons, reasons. Why would anyone want to be bald? I don't ever want to be bald."

Granny Mary smiled warmly and said, "You know, some people lose their hair because of a poor diet. So, for example, if you do not get enough vitamin D from your food and sunlight, you can suffer hair loss. Vitamin D deficiency in young children also causes a disease known as rickets, which causes the bones to be soft and weak, and sometimes bend."

"Wow, I didn't know that," Penny said, clearly surprised.

"Yes, so make sure you eat your greens," Granny Mary said while laughing.

Granny Mary gathered herself, and continued, "Sometimes, the chemicals in hair products can destroy the hair and scalp and result in hair loss. Relaxers or perms contain chemicals like sodium hydroxide (lye), potassium hydroxide, lithium hydroxide, guanidine hydroxide, and ammonium thioglycolate (known as perm salt). If the relaxers are left in the hair for too long, the chemicals in them, especially lye, can cause severe burns to the scalp and hair loss."

Interrupting Granny Mary's attempt to continue her mini lecture, Penny raised her hand and began speaking. "Granny Mary, do you remember Andrea, who used to go to McKenzie High School? She has bald patches. The sides of her head are nyampy-nyampy (patchy)."

Granny Mary nodded and said, "I know her. Well, you see, some women also suffer hair loss because they wear hairstyles that put constant pressure on their hair follicles. I know of many women who suffered hair loss from consistently wearing tight box braids or glued in weaves. Hair loss that comes from putting pressure on the hair follicles is called traction alopecia."

Granny Mary looked up at the roof, as if searching for thoughts up there. She quickly continued, "Sometimes, people are bald because baldness is a cultural norm or requirement."

"Like something everyone in the community does?" Penny asked.

Granny Mary replied, "Pretty much. Remember we talked about the Maasai men having long hair? Well, Maasai women generally have shaved heads. Also, in some parts of Africa, widows are required to have their heads shaved, as part of traditional mourning rituals. This practice makes many women feel sad and abused."

"Ooh, ooh, I know what a widow is," Penny interjected. "A widow is a woman whose husband died."

Granny Mary nodded in agreement and said, "That is correct, sweet pea."

Granny Mary turns page to reveal another photo.

Figure 32

"She's pretty!" Penny exclaimed.

"Yes, she is," Granny Mary said. "Some people also lose their hair because of diseases, or the medicines they use to treat diseases like cancer, high blood pressure, arthritis, depression, and heart disease. In the United States, Congresswoman Ayana Pressley is bald. She serves the 7th Congressional District of the state of Massachusetts. Ayana Pressley is bald because she has a disease called alopecia, which causes the immune system to destroy the hair follicles and make the hair fall out. Because the hair often falls out in patches, some people with alopecia would shave off all their hair. Congresswoman Ayana Pressley wore box braids and other hairstyles before she finally decided to go completely bald, and publicly discuss her battle with alopecia. So, you see, you never really know why someone is bald."

"Or why they wear other hairstyles," Penny interjected.

"That's true," Granny Mary said. "You never really know."

Right then, Penny threw up her hands and shouted, "Whew! Granny, that's a lot of beautiful hair!"

Granny Mary leaned back in her chair and spoke softly and confidently, "Yes, indeed. The texture of Black hair allows it to be a lot of magic and do a lot of magic. Black hair is magic."

Penny chuckled and replied, "No, it's eclectic."

Granny Mary smiled and said, "Indeed it is!"

Granny Mary looked at Penny and said, "We should get up and stretch, we've been sitting for a while."

Granny Mary and Penny stood up, stretched their hands to the ceiling, and then bent over and touched their toes for several minutes. Penny then stood up and started doing jumping jacks. Granny Mary smiled.

Chapter 6

Eclectic Hair Can do Things

Adornment and Beauty

Figure 33

Granny Mary sat down and said, "Let's have some more tea and gyaff about some of the functions of eclectic hair. You know, the purpose of some of these hairstyles. We'll revisit some of the styles we already talked about."

Granny Mary continued, "Well, my dear, Black hair is eclectic because Black hair and hairstyles serve many different functions. Many of the hairstyles are just for beauty or fashion; people wear them because they think it makes them look attractive. In pre-colonial Africa, people added beads, grass, twigs, yarn, and other objects to the hair. Today, a lot of parents still dress up their daughters' hair with bubblies (hair bubbles) and slides (barrettes), just like this little girl."

"Did you wear bubblies and slides when you were a little girl?" Penny asked.

"Yes," replied Granny Mary. "When we were growing up, our parents used to cover our head with slides and bubblies. Our heads used to look like Christmas trees. Worse, those things used to hurt our heads when we tried to sleep with them." Granny Mary threw back her head and laughed heartily.

Granny Mary turned the page.

"That looks like snail shells," Penny said, staring at the photo.

Figure 34

Granny Mary tilted her head to the side while looking at the photo, and said, "It actually does."

Granny Mary leaned over the table and continued her lesson. She said, "These are cowrie shells and Black people use them to adorn their hair. The woman with box braids had cowries in her hair (**Fig. 27**) The cowrie is the shell of a sea snail. The word cowrie comes from the Hindi word 'kaudi' (or kaudee), which means penny, and from 'kaparda,' the Sanskrit word for cowry shell. The cowrie shell was once used as a form of currency (or money) in pre-colonial Africa and around the world; so, people showed off their wealth by wearing cowrie shells in the hair and on the body. In pre-colonial Africa, cowrie shells were also used in divination, to predict the future. Today, medicine men and women in Africa still use cowrie shells for divination, and some Black people also wear cowrie shells to show pride in their African heritage, but cowries are no longer a sign of wealth. In fact, nowadays there are fake cowrie shells that are made of plastic."

Timesaver

"What else can eclectic hair do?" Penny asked.

Granny Mary said, "Well, we kind of talked about this in passing, but our eclectic hair is a time-saver. Hairstyles like locs, braids, weaves, wigs, and threaded hair, keeps the hair in place for a long time, so you don't have to worry about combing or styling your hair every day."

"But people with free hair don't have to spend a lot of time combing their hair because free or wild *is* the style," Penny said.

Granny Mary and Penny laughed.

"When I was growing up in Sandvoort Village, Sunday was braiding day," Granny Mary began. "If you passed by any house on Sunday evening, you would see a young girl sitting on the steps, between the legs of another girl or woman, who was braiding her hair. We braided our hair for the week. Sunday braiding was a cultural ritual that allowed us to bond with each other, learn from each other, and to pass on information and skills to future generations. At nights, we tied our heads with head-ties to prevent our hair from getting messy."

Penny interjected and said, "I use a head-tie at night, but my hair still looks like a wild bush in the morning. Mommy said it's because I roll around too much when I sleep."

Granny Mary laughed lustily, and then said, "That happens to the best of us." She continued, "Anyway, some Black people wear certain hairstyles because they want their hair to stay in place so they can look organized or professional. Some people think that straight or organized hair is more professional, so they create those hairstyles to go to work, church, and other important places. Black people's rejection of natural Black hair is often the result of religious and cultural teachings that taught them to see African things as deficient. Even Madam C. J. Walker created products to help Black women 'manage' their hair."

Protection

"Anyway, my love, let's continue," Granny Mary said. "Many eclectic hairstyles protect the hair from damage or harsh weather. Box braids, threading, wigs, and other styles that cover the natural, can protect the hair from damage and harsh weather, when they do not put excess stress on the hair. For example, in the winter, the cold temperature makes the hair dry and brittle and causes it to break, even when it's moisturized. The extreme heat of Guyana and other tropical regions can also damage the hair by making it dry and brittle. So, the additions protect the hair from damage, just like the *otjize* paste protect the hair and skin of the Himba (OvaHimba) people."

Receptacle

Figure 35

Granny Mary turned the page of the album.

Penny looked stunned. "Is she putting things in that lady's hair?" She asked.

Granny Mary laughed, and replied. "Yes, she is. You see, honey, sometimes eclectic hair is used as a receptacle."

Penny repeated quietly, "Receptacle, receptacle."

Granny Mary interjected, "Yes, a receptable; something that is used to hold things. You know, like a container. During enslavement, many African people were captured from the continent of African and taken all over the world to work on rice plantations, sugar plantations, cotton plantations, and in many other areas. It is said that enslaved Africans in the Caribbean, the United States, and in other parts of the world braided rice, seeds, jewelry, and other items into their hair to ensure they had food and other kinds of security in times of uncertainty."

Penny looked up at Granny Mary and asked, "Were you a slave, Granny Mary?" Did you hide things in your hair?"

Before she could continue with her litany of questions, Granny Mary responded, "Well, I wasn't enslaved, but my grandmother was, and she may have hidden things in her hair. You know, my mother told me that she used to hide her money in her hair to prevent bullies from taking it away. I also used to hide my money in my hair when I wanted to play but didn't have pockets to secure it. By putting my money in my hair, I was able to play without losing it."

"Do you have to have a special hairstyle to hide things in your hair?" Penny asked.

"Not really," Granny Mary replied. "But some hairstyles are better for holding objects and keeping them in place. Cornrows, threaded hair, and plaits are some of the best hairstyles for holding things in place."

"What other things can eclectic hair do?" Penny inquired.

Granny Mary paused and, once again, looked up to the ceiling.

Make a statement/Send a Message

"Ah, yes!" She said, "Sometimes eclectic hair is used to make a statement."

"Do you mean 'to say something specific'? Like, to send a message?" Penny asked.

Granny Mary nodded vigorously and replied, "Yes, bright girl. Sometimes, we use our hairstyles to send general or specific messages to those around us. In pre-colonial Africa, certain hairstyles and adornments were associated with particular deities or gods. For instance, some female traditional healers wore a threaded hairstyle that was upraised and ran along the center of the head, like a rooster's comb."

"So, people from those African societies could 'read' a person's hairstyle and tell who they were?" Penny queried.

"Exactly!" Granny replied.

To fit in and stand out

Penny smiled and asked, "That's amazing! Is that all, Granny Mary?"

"No, dear," Granny Mary responded. "But we're winding down. Let's talk about how eclectic hair helps us to fit in. You see, sometimes people wear their hair in particular ways because they believe it will help them to fit in with certain groups. Sometimes, Black people wear straightened hair because they think it makes them look more professional. Some people also think that natural hair, free hair, or other hairstyles that are fuzzy, are not professional. Some even prefer hairstyles that look more like White people's hair."

Penny interjected, "But natural hair is not always free or 'wild.' Plus, you could still look professional with natural hairstyles."

"That's true," Granny Mary said. "But remember, sometimes Black people also wear their hair in certain styles because they want to fit in with Black people who embrace their African heritage. Those individuals sometimes get in trouble at work if their jobs have rules against certain kinds of hair."

"So, then, hair can help you fit into different kinds of groups?" Penny thought out loud.

"Exactly!" Granny Mary said, nodding in agreement.

"That's confusing. How can you tell which group a person is trying to fit into?" Penny inquired.

"You can observe them to try to figure out what kinds of groups or associations they belong to," Granny Mary responded. "However, to be certain, you have to let people tell you if they are wearing their hairstyle to fit in, to stand out, or for some other reason."

Penny smiled mischievously, then said, "This was a great discussion-lecture, Granny Mary, but my brain is tired now."

To find our way

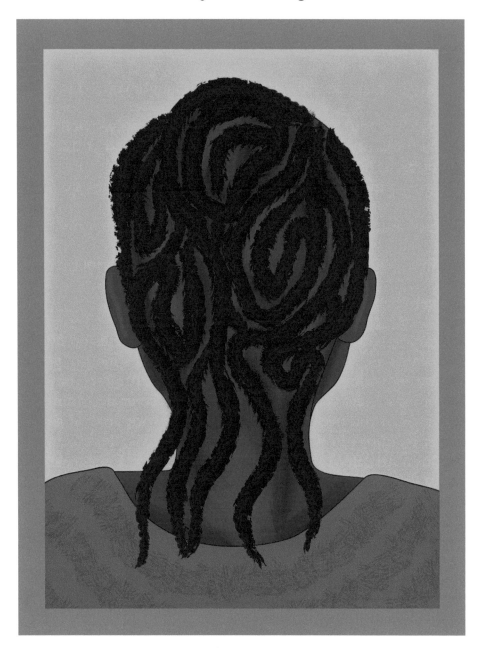

Figure 36

Granny Mary laughed and replied, "Ok, love. We'll wrap up soon, but I want to tell you about one last function of eclectic hair. Maps!"

Granny Mary turned the page

Trying to bring the hair talk to a speedy conclusion, Penny said, "Those are just cornrows, Granny Mary."

Granny Mary retorted, "Not just cornrows. Maps. Through oral narratives, we learn that during enslavement, Black people often plotted and escaped from bondage. Sometimes, they braided escape routes into women's hair to help them remember the directions. So, the cornrows were maps. Therefore, cornrowed hair had multiple functions at the same time."

"Granny Mary, I have a question, sort of," Penny stated.

Granny Mary laughed heartily, then said, "I thought you said your brain is tired."

Penny slid down onto her chair and laughed heartily. "Well, it kinda is. But I remembered something about hair I wanted to tell you. Did you know that Trevor's mother got in trouble at her job because she went to work with natural free hair? He said that his mother's manager told her to 'Go home and don't come back until you tame that wild bush.' But that's not fair. Even though he's a pest, his mother's manager shouldn't insult her hair or send her home. Do you think that's right, Granny Mary?"

"Well, Granny Mary began, "When yuh haan in tigah mout', pat he head.'"

"Pardon me?" Penny responded.

Granny Mary laughed and explained, "That's a Guyanese proverb. In Standard English, it's translated as, 'When your hand is in the tiger's mouth, you should pat his head.' That means that sometimes, when a more powerful force or person threatens your livelihood or existence, you should try to appease or accommodate them until you can do better. So, if you need that job to survive, work around the rules until you can do better. For example, in the United States, Mr. Tyler Perry owns his own 330-acre movie studio in Atlanta, Georgia. Before he became a successful media mogul, he had to play by the rules of others. Today, he can do whatever he likes because he is his own boss."

Penny smiled and said, "So, his hand is not in the tiger's mouth."

"Correct," Granny Mary said. "One day, Black hair will be understood and appreciated by Black people and others, but until then, we must educate ourselves and others, and wear our hair proudly."

"So, we don't have to change Black hair, only bad thoughts and attitudes towards Black hair," Penny mused.

"That's an excellent way of thinking about it," Granny Mary responded.

Granny Mary leaned back in her chair, crossed her legs, and breathed a sigh of relief that her mini lecture was almost over. After a few minutes, she looked at Penny and said, "You see, sweetie pie, Black hair will always be an important part of our history, culture, and identity. Diverse Black hairstyles are also celebrated by famous Black people from every segment of society and seen on Facebook, Instagram, YouTube, and every type of visual media. Do you remember *The Black Panther* movie?"

Penny said, "Of course, Granny Mary! I watched it about five times already. Daddy and mommy have the DVD of it. There's a lot of eclectic hair in that movie! Some women even have bald heads!"

"Indeed!" Granny Mary said. "When the Black Panther movie was released in 2018, eclectic natural hair was on full display in all its glory. For example, Shuri (Guyana-born Letitia Wright), the younger sister of King T'Challa, wore box braids with extensions; King T'Challa/The Black Panther(Chadwick Boseman) had low contoured hair; the Dora Milaje warriors had bald heads; Nakia (Lupita Nyong'o) had low-cut hair, styled in 'Wakanda knots,' which resemble Bantu knots, but are looser; Kilmonger (Michael B. Jordan) had short micro dreads on the top half of his head; and Queen Mother Ramonda (Angela Bassett), had white micro locs (sister locs), which were generally covered throughout the film with the traditional Zulu headdress of married women called *isicholo.*"

Clearly relieved, Penny threw up her two hands in the hair and declared, "Wow, Granny Mary, we have covered a world of hair! Now we're at the end of our hair journey."

Granny Mary smiled, closed the album, and said, "Yes, my sweet Penny! We can never cover ALL of the amazing hairstyles and functions of eclectic Black hair, but I want you to remember that your hair, our hair, Black hair is beautiful and unique. Black hair is many different things. Black hair can do ALL kinds of amazing things!"

Penny jumped out of her chair, clapped her hands and said, "Amen to that! It's ECLECTIC!!!"

Penny and Granny Mary burst into uproarious laughter.

Granny Mary then walked around the table with her arms opened wide. Penny quickly finished her tea and rushed in for a hug.

As she readied herself to leave Granny Mary's home, Penny quickly turned around and said, "Granny Mary, will you tell me more about your blue hands one of these days?"

"Of course, pumpkin. Our next gyaff session will be about 'blue hands.'"

Penny scampered out the door, chanting, "It's eclectic! It's eclectic! It's eclectic!"

Glossary

1. **African villages in Guyana**: Africans in Guyana purchased land and established villages after they were emancipated from enslavement.

2. **afro**: A word that was derived from the term Afro-American. It is a round-shaped hairstyle that is created with natural hair.

3. **afro comb**: A long-toothed, fork-like comb that is used to comb out the afro hairstyle. The afro comb is also a symbol of Black identity, especially the comb with the fist on it.

4. **Alexander Godefroy**: The French hairstylist who invented the hair dryer in 1890. That earlier version of the hairdryer had a bonnet that was connected to a gas stove via its chimney pipe.

5. **alopecia**: A type of hair loss that develops when the hair follicles are damaged, either by an autoimmune condition or by stress placed on the hair.

6. **ancestor**: Forefather or foremother. A person from whom one is descended.

7. **Angola**: Officially known as the Republic of Angola is a country in western part of southern Africa.

8. **Archaeology**: the study of human history and prehistory through examination, and interpretation of excavated artifacts and other physical remains. In the United States, archaeology is one of the four branches of anthropology.

9. **balata:** The gum or sap that comes from the bulletwood tree is called balata, a kind of natural rubber or latex that was used to make rubber balls and other items.

10. **Bantu**: The Bantu-speaking people are from the Niger-Congo region of Central and Southern Africa. The Bantu people belong to more than four hundred ethnic groups and speak more than five hundred different Bantu languages, such as Swahili, Xhosa, and Zulu.

11. **bauxite**: A sedimentary rock that is used to produce aluminum.

12. **beret**: A soft, round hat with a flat crown, often woven or knitted.

13. **black cake**: Also known as rum cake, this is a dark fruit cake that is made different types of dried fruits, burnt brown sugar, wine, and other ingredients.

14. **Black Power Movement**: A movement in the 1960s and 1970s that promoted racial pride, economic empowerment, and self-reliance.

15. **Blaxploitation films**: Produced in the 1970s in the United States, these films often portrayed negative stereotypes of Black people, such as gangster and thief.

16. **Bu'n Down House [burn down house]**: A Guyanese game that involves two teams, who work to conquer each other's territory by taking long jumps. A person from one team is blindfolded, tapped in the palm of the hand by a member of the opposing team, and then required to identify the person from the other team that touched them. A correct identification allows the previously blindfolded person to jump forward in the direction of the other team. When a member of the opposing team jumps over the boundary line of the other team, they have successfully bu'n down (burned down) that teams house.

17. **bush tea**: Herbal teas that are made with the leaves, fruits, barks, and roots of trees. Some common types of bush tea include lemon grass, daisy, conga pump, sweet broom, and sweet sage. Bush teas are also often used as medicines to cure fevers, colds, and other illnesses.

18. **canerows**: Another word used for cornrows.

19. **Chinese skipping**: This is Chinese jump rope. Two players stand with a circular stretchy rope at their ankles so that it is taut. A jumper then jumps with legs together and apart as the players spell out different words. The player cannot pause or hit the rope with their legs. Each time the jumper successfully clears a level, the rope is raised to the knees, waist, shoulders, and even neck.

20. **circumvent**: To find a way around an obstacle or problem.

21. **Civil Rights Movement**: A movement that took place in the 1950s and 1960s, which captured the struggle for Black people to gain equal rights.

22. **Common Entrance**: A group of examinations that children in Guyana in Guyana and the Caribbean must take in order to gain entrance into high chool.

23. **cookup rice**: A Guyanese cuisine made with rice, peas, coconut milk, and diverse spices and meats.

24. **cowrie shells**: The cowrie is the shell of a sea snail. The word cowrie comes from the Hindi word 'kaudi' (or kaudee), which means penny, and from 'kaparda,'

the Sanskrit word for cowry shell. The cowrie shell was once used as a form of currency (or money) in pre-colonial Africa and around the world.

25. **creamy crack**: This term refers to the danger and addictive nature of relaxer cream or perm.

26. **Creolese**: Guyana's creole language. A creole language is a language that was created from the blending of two or more languages over a long period of time.

27. **crimping iron/crimper**: A hair iron with two metal plates that have crests (peaks) and troughs (indentations) and used to give the hair a wavy appearance.

28. **curling iron**: A cylindrical hair iron with a long barrel-like body that is used to curl the hair.

29. **dashiki**: a colourful top worn in Africa. During the Civil Rights and Black Power Movements, Black people around the world wore dashikis to show African pride. Today, dashikis are word on an everyday basis, and sometimes by people who are not of African descent.

30. **Demerara River**: A 216-mile-long freshwater river in Guyana.

31. **Dougla**: A mixed raced person in Guyana, usually of African and East Indian heritage.

32. **eclectic**: Something that is derived from a wide range of sources.

33. **enculturation**: The social process by which culture is learned and transmitted across generations (Kottak 2015).

34. **exposition**: A detailed description or explanation of a concept.

35. **flabbergasted**: To be shocked or astonished.

36. **flat iron**: A hair iron with two flat metal plates on each clamp, which is used to straighten the hair.

37. **frond**: Leaf or fern.

38. **Gabriel Kazanjian**: He patented the first hair dryer in the United States.

39. **Garrett Augustus Morgan**: He is credited with accidentally inventing the first hair straightening cream.

40. **gele**: a kind of head-tie worn by West African women.

41. **Geri Cusenza**: He invented modern-day crimper in 1972 to design the hair of legendary American singer Barbara Streisand.

42. **Guyana**: The only English-speaking sovereign nation on the continent of South America.

43. **gyaff**: To chat (in Creolese).

44. **Haile Selassie**: Emperor of Ethiopia from 1930-1974.

45. **hair grease**: shea butter, petroleum jelly, and other kinds of hair products used to moisturize the hair and scalp and prevent the hair from becoming too dry and brittle and breaking.

46. **hassa**: a kind of catfish that lives in the muddy bottoms of trenches, rivers, swamps, and streams, and other bodies of fresh water.

47. **hassa-back**: French cornrows or inverted Dutch cornrows.

48. **Henry M. Childrey**: He and Samuel H. Bundles Jr. (both African Americans) first patented the long-teeth afro comb in 1960.

49. **Himba (Ova-Hima)**: an ethnic group in Africa that live in northern Namibia and Southern Angola on the continent of Africa.

50. **hunter-gatherers** (foragers): People who get food by hunting animals, fishing, gathering edible plants. They are nomadic, moving from one place to the next in search of game, edible plants, and waterways.

51. *ifari apakan*: half-shaved head word by the *ilari* (messengers) of the *Oba* (king) among the Yoruba of Nigeria.

52. **Igbo**: an ethnic group that mostly reside in Southeastern Nigeria.

53. **ilari**: messengers of the *Oba* (king) among the Yoruba of Nigeria.

54. **irun kiko**: In Yoruba, *irun* means 'hair' and *kiko* means 'gather'; so *irun kiko* literally means 'gathered hair' or 'threaded hair.'

55. **Isaac K. Shero**: he patented the first flat iron in 1909.

56. **isi**: head (in Igbo language).

57. **isicholo**: traditional headdress of married Zulu women.

58. **isi owu**: *Isi* (ee-see) means 'head' and *owu* (oh-woo) means 'cotton' or 'thread.' So, *isi owu* literally means threaded head, referring to the hairstyle.

59. **iyawo**: wife (in Yoruba language).

60. **jheri curl**: a type of hair processing that creates large waves or curls in Black woolly hair. It consists of creams, conditioners and moisturizers. It was created by American chemist Robert William Redding, nicknamed "Jheri."

61. **Kenya**: Officially named the Republic of Kenya, this country is located in Eastern Africa.

62. **Lessons**: After-school tutoring. Children in Guyana often to go lessons when they are preparing for major exams like Common Entrance, the high school entrance exam.

63. **libation**: offering to a deity or ancestor, usually in the form of a drink.

64. **Maasai**: an ethnic group in the African country of Kenya.

65. **Madam C. J. Walker**: Legally named Sarah Breedlove, she was listed in the Guinness Book of World Records as the first female millionaire in the United States of America. She marketed cosmetics and hair products for Black hair created the Madam C. J. Walker Manufacturing Company.

66. **Marcel Grateau**: A French hairdresser named Marcel Grateau who began using heated metals, like the hot comb, to straighten the hair in the 1870s.

67. **Masquerade**: Elaborate performances, ceremonies, or plays that tell stories about the people who participate in them. Masquerades have performers who wear masks and other types of costumes that hide their identities.

68. **meh-cheh meh-cheh**: A Creolese term that references "this and that," "tids and bits," a conflation of mismatched elements, or nonsense.

69. **micro locs (sister locs/mister locs)**: smaller, more organized locs.

70. **moran**: A term used for warriors among the Maasai of Kenya in Eastern Africa.

71. **Namibia**: Officially named the Republic of Namibia, this is a country in southern Africa.

72. **Natty dread**: A term used to refer to Rastas (Rastafarians) and thick dreadlocks they wear. Natty dread is also the title of the seventh album released by the late musician Bob Marley, one of the most visible Rastas.

73. **Nazarite vow**: In the Hebrew Bible, it was vow taken voluntarily by Hebrew people. A person who took the Nazarite vow was required to abstain from drinking wine, eating anything that grows on a vine (like grapes), and cutting their hair.

74. **Nemesis**: An adversary, competitor, or opponent.

75. **Nigeria**: A country in West African and the African country that currently has the largest population.

76. **nuclear family**: A family consisting of two parents and their children.

77. **nyampy-nyampy**: Means patchy in Creolese.

78. **Oba**: Means king among the Yoruba of Nigeria.

79. **ochre**: A type of clay.

80. **Omuzumba**: A type of plant that produces the perfumed resin that gives the *otjize* paste a sweet smell.

81. **onigi**: Means 'sticks' Yoruba language.

82. **oral narratives**: Stories that are passed down through word of mouth.

83. **orishas** Deities in the syncretic Santería religion that emerged among slaves in Cuba.

84. **othermother**: Women who informally adopt children and assume responsibility for their economic providence, discipline, personal care, and other factors associated with child rearing, even when the children continue to live with their *bloodmothers* (biological mothers) or other *consanguineal kin* (blood relatives).

85. **otjize**: A mixture of butterfat and the reddish *ochre* (a type of clay).

86. **owu** (oh-woo): Means 'cotton' or 'thread' in Igbo language.

87. **pastoralist**: People who herd livestock like cattle and goats for food and other resources, such as the Himba (OvaHimba).

88. **pepperpot**: Guyana's national dish. It is like a dark brown stew that is made with various types of meats and spices, and boiled in cassava cassareep, which gives the stew its brown colour.

89. **raffia palm**: A type of palm tree in Africa. The fronds are used to style the hair and create the skirts of masquerades.

90. **Ras Tafar I Makonen**: The pre-coronation name of Haile Selassie, Emperor of Ethiopia from 1930-1974.

91. **Rastafarian/Rasta**: A religion that was started in Jamaica and the Caribbean, and later, spread to the rest of the world. Rastafari has many other beliefs, but dreadlocks is one of the most visible symbols of their identity."

92. **receptacle**: an object used to hold something else.

93. **ring games**: Guyanese children play many games that require them to form a circle, such as "coloured girl in the ring," "ring around the rosey," "Limbo, limbo Sah-lay," "jumbie leff 'e pipe hey" and "I lost my belt on a Saturday night."

94. **rites of passage**: rituals and customs associated with the transition from one state of life to the next. For example, marriage ceremonies help a person to go from being single to married.

95. **Samuel H. Bundles Jr.**: He and Henry M. Childrey (both African Americans) first patented the long-teeth afro comb in 1960.

96. **Sandvoort Village**: An African village in West Canje region in the county of Berbice in Guyana.

97. **Sango**: A deity in the Yoruba pantheon.

98. **Saul Out**: A Guyanese game that is played outdoors with two teams. Vertical and horizontal dars (bars or columns) and boxes are drawn on the ground. One team guards the dars as the other team attempts to run through the figure on the ground from one end to the next, without being tapped or slapped by a member of the opposing team. Any runner that is tapped or slapped by a while running through the figure gets out of the game. A team wins when the last runner from the team gets to the other side safely.

99. **senseh fowl**: a chicken that has sparse, ruffled feathers.

100. **Soul Train**: A music-dance television program that ran from 1971 to 2006.

101. **Sumptuary Laws**: Laws that limited the consumption of food, clothing, and other items, in order to prevent extravagance. However, during enslavement, Sumptuary laws were really meant to maintain the social structure of society and keep Black women separated from Whites, and subjugated.

102. **synthetic**: something that is 'fake' or imitates something real or genuine.

103. **Tanzania**: Officially named the United Republic of Tanzania, this is an African country in East Africa.

104. **The CROWN Act**: Stands for "Creating a Respectful and Open World for Natural Hair." The Crown Act was first introduced in California and became a law on July 3, 2019.

105. **Tignon**: Sometimes called 'tiyon,' is a kind of head covering that resembles the *gele* (head-tie), worn by West African women.

106. **Tignon Laws**: Enacted in 1786 by Governor Don Estevan Miró of New Orleans, Louisiana, United States of America. Tignon Laws were instituted to prevent Black women and other women of colour from dressing and behaving too flamboyantly.

107. **traction alopecia**: Hair loss that comes from putting pressure on the hair follicles.

108. **uri**: A type of fruit. The juice from the *uri* fruit was used to dye the raffia frond black.

109. **Yoruba**: An ethnic group in Nigeria. Yoruba people mostly live in the southwestern region of Nigeria.

Works Cited

Bundles, Alelia. *On Her Own Ground: The Life and Times of Madam C.J. Walker*. New York: Scribner, 2001.

Bush, Barbara. *Slave Women in Caribbean Society:1650-1838*. Bloomington: Indiana University Press, 1990.

Close, Stacey K. 2015. Chapter 5 "Nearer to Thee: Old Women in the Quarters." In *Elderly Slaves of the Plantation South,* pp. 63-78. Abingdon, Oxford: Taylor & Francis, 2015.

Collins, Patricia Hill. "Bloodmothers, Othermothers, and Women-Centered Networks." In *Reconstructing Gender: A Multicultural Anthology*, 3rd ed. Edited by Estelle Disch, 317-323. Boston: McGraw-Hill, 2003.

Cowling, Camilla, Diana Paton, Emily West, Maria Helena Pereira Toledo Machado, eds. *Motherhood, Childlessness and the Care of Children in Atlantic Slave Societies*, 2020.

Cutrufelli, Mari Rosa. *Women of Africa: Roots of Oppression*. London: Zed Press, 1983.

Dabiri, Emma. *Twisted: The Tangled History of Black Hair Culture*. New York: Harper Perennial, 2020.

Gillespie, Catherine Clinton Michele. *The Devil's Lane: Sex and Race in the Early South*. Oxford: Oxford University Pressm, 1997.

Jiminez, Jillian. 2002. "The History of Grandmothers in the African-American Community." *Social Service Review, vol.* 76, no. 4, 2002, pp. 523-551.

Johnson, Elizabeth, Dr. *Resistance and Empowerment in Black Women's Hair Styling*. Burlington, VT: Ashgate Publishing Limited, 2013.

Jones, Monique L. *The Book of Awesome Black Americans: Scientific Pioneers, Trailblazing Entrepreneurs, Barrier-Breaking Activists and Afro-Futurists*. Coral Gables, Florida: Mango Media. New York: McGraw-Hill Education, 2019.

Kottak, Conrad Phillip. *Cultural Anthropology: Appreciating Human Diversity.* New York: McGraw-Hill Education, 2015.

Tulloch, Carol. "The resounding power of the Afro comb." *In* Hair: Styling Culture and Fashion. G. Biddle-Perry and S. Cheang, (eds.). Pp. 124-38. New York and Oxford: Berg, 2008.

Winters, Lisa Ze. The Mulatta Concubine: Terror, Intimacy, Freedom, and Desire in the Black Transatlantic. Athens: University of Georgia Press, 2016.

Bibliography

Adichie, Chimamanda Ngozi. *Americanah: A Novel.* New York: Random House, 2013.

Antiri, Janet Adwoa. "Akan Combs." *African Arts,* vol. 8, no. 1, 1974, pp. 32-35.

Ashton, Sally-Ann. *Origins of the Afro Comb: 6,000 Years of Culture, Politics and Identity.* Cambridge: The Fitzwilliam Museum, 2013.

Ashton, Sally-Ann. "Combs." *Origins of the Afro Comb,* https://www.fitzmuseum.cam.ac.uk/gallery/afrocombs/combs/index.html, accessed December 6, 2020.

Ashton, Sally-Ann. "Radical Objects: The Black Fist Afro Comb." *History Workshop,* 10 February 2014, https://www.historyworkshop.org.uk/radical-objects-the-black-fist-afro-comb/, accessed December 10, 2020.

Batulukisi, Niangi and Gert Morreel and Joachim Neugroschel. *Hair in African Art and Culture.* London, UK: Museum for African Art, 2000.

Bundles, Alelia. *On Her Own Ground: The Life and Times of Madam C.J. Walker.* New York: Scribner, 2001.

Bundles, A'Lelia. 2020. Self Made: Inspired by the Life of Madam C.J. Walker.

Bush, Barbara. *Slave Women in Caribbean Society:1650-1838.* Bloomington: Indiana University Press, 1990.

Byrd, Ayana and Lori Tharps. *Hair Story: Untangling The Roots of Black Hair in America,* 2nd ed. New York: St. Martin's Griffin, 2014.

Cabrera, Cozbi A. *My Hair is a Garden.* Park Ridge, Illinois: Albert Whitman & Company, 2018.

Chimbiri, K.N. *Secrets of the Afro Comb: 6,000 Years of Art and Culture.* London: Golden Destiny Ltd.

Close, Stacey K. 2015. Chapter 5 "Nearer to Thee: Old Women in the Quarters." In *Elderly Slaves of the Plantation South,* pp. 63-78. Abingdon, Oxford: Taylor & Francis, 2015.

Collins, Patricia Hill. "Bloodmothers, Othermothers, and Women-Centered Networks." In *Reconstructing Gender: A Multicultural Anthology*, 3rd ed. Edited by Estelle Disch, 317-323. Boston: McGraw-Hill, 2003.

Cutrufelli, Mari Rosa. *Women of Africa: Roots of Oppression*. London: Zed Press, 1983.

Dabiri, Emma. *Twisted: The Tangled History of Black Hair Culture*. New York: Harper Perennial, 2020.

Gabara, Princess. 2017. "The History of the Afro." https://www.ebony.com/style/the-history-of-the-afro/, accessed November 24, 2020.

Gillespie, Catherine Clinton Michele. *The Devil's Lane: Sex and Race in the Early South*. Oxford: Oxford University Pressm, 1997.

Gittens, Sandra. "An overview of African type hair for the Afro comb project." *In* Origins of the Afro Comb. Sally-Ann Ashton, ed. Pp. 20-23. Cambridge: The Fitzwilliam Museum.

"Jheri Curl, Conk, Dreadlocks & Afro." *Jazma Hair, Inc.*, 1999, www.jazma.com/black-hair-history. Accessed December 19, 2020.

Jiminez, Jillian. 2002. "The History of Grandmothers in the African-American Community." *Social Service Review, vol.* 76, no. 4, 2002, pp. 523-551.

Johnson, Elizabeth, Dr. *Resistance and Empowerment in Black Women's Hair Styling*. Burlington, VT: Ashgate Publishing Limited, 2013.

Jones, Monique L. *The Book of Awesome Black Americans: Scientific Pioneers, Trailblazing Entrepreneurs, Barrier-Breaking Activists and Afro-Futurists*. Coral Gables, Florida: Mango Media. New York: McGraw-Hill Education, 2019.

Kottak, Conrad Phillip. *Cultural Anthropology: Appreciating Human Diversity*. New York: McGraw-Hill Education, 2015.

Kwami, A. "Drawing a comb." *In* Origins of the Afro Comb. Sally-Ann Ashton, ed. Pp. 30-33. Cambridge: The Fitzwilliam Museum, 2014.

Lawal, Babatunde. 2000. "Orilonise: The Hermeneutics of the Head and Hairstyles Among the Yoruba." *In* Hair in African Art and Culture. Frank Herreman, ed. Pg. 97. Prestel.

Mack, Bayer, Director. 2019. *No Lye: An American Beauty Story*. Produced by Bayer Mack and Frances Presley-Rice, Distributed by Block Starz Music Television, 55 minutes.

Marriott, Kaya .2019. "30 Awesome Picture Books Uplifting Black Kids with Natural Hair." *Comfy Girl with Curls,* 22 July 2019, https://www.comfygirlwithcurls.com/2019/07/22/childrens-books-black-kids-natural-hair/, accessed December 9, 2020.

Martin, Chrystal. 2018. "How 'Black Panther' Got Its Gorgeous Afrocentric Hair" https://www.nytimes.com/2018 /02/14/style/black-panther-natural-hair.html, accessed December 22, 2020.

McMillan, M. "Good hair/bad hair: Black styling, culture and politics in the African Diaspora." *In* Origins of the Afro Comb. Sally-Ann Ashton, ed. Pp. 48-59. Cambridge: The Fitzwilliam Museum, 2014.

Moffitt, Kimberly Dr. The Black Hair Syllabus, https://www.blackhairsyllabus.com/, accessed November 27, 2020.

Nelson, Jimmy. "Before they Pass Away." New York: teNeues Publishing, 2013.

Olupona, Busayo. "The Art of African Hair Threading." *Busayo,* 14 September 2019, https://www.busayonyc.com/the-art-of-african-hair-threading/, date accessed, November 19, 2020.

Randle, Brenda A. "I am not my Hair: African American Women and their Struggles with Embracing Natural Hair." *Race, Gender & Class,* vol. 22, no.1-2, 2015, pp.114-121.

Richards-Greaves, Gillian. Chapter 3 "Wipin', Winin', and Wukkin': Constructing, Contesting, and Displaying Gender Values." *Rediasporization: African-Guyanese Kweh-Kweh.* Jackson: University Press of Mississippi, 2020.

Robinson, Phoebe. *You Can't Touch My Hair: And Other Things I Still Have to Explain.* New York: Plume, 2016.

Rock, Chris. 2009. *Good Hair.* Documentary Film. Jeff Stilson, Director. Chris Rock Entertainment.

Sagay, Esi. African Hairstyles: Styles of Yesterday and Today. New York: Pearson Education, 1983.

Sieber, Roy and Frank Herreman, eds. *Hair in African Art and Culture* (New York.

Spear, Thomas and Richard Waller, eds. *Being Maasai: Ethnicity and Identity in East Africa.* Athens: Ohio University Press, 1993.

"The Crown Act." https://www.thecrownact.com, accessed December 23, 2020.

Tulloch, Carol. "The resounding power of the Afro comb." *In* Hair: Styling Culture and Fashion. G. Biddle-Perry and S. Cheang, (eds.). Pp. 124-38. New York and Oxford: Berg, 2008.

Shuiaa, Mwalimu J. and Kenya J. Shuiaa. *The SAGE Encyclopedia of African Cultural Heritage in North America.* Thousand Oaks, CA: SAGE Publications, Inc, 2015.

Uwalaka, Merlin 2018. "Black Hair History." https://www.merlinuwalaka.com/blog/black-history-hair, accessed November 27, 2020.

White, Shane and Graham White. "Slave Hair and African American Culture in the Eighteenth and Nineteenth Centuries." *Journal of Southern History*, vol. 61, no.1, 1995, p.72.

Winters, Lisa Ze. The Mulatta Concubine: Terror, Intimacy, Freedom, and Desire in the Black Transatlantic. Athens: University of Georgia Press, 2016.

CPSIA information can be obtained
at www.ICGtesting.com
Printed in the USA
BVHW020436170321
602670BV00003B/15